HOUSES REBORN

Houses of the Dead Volume 3

LEAH R CUTTER

Knotted Road Press

Houses Reborn
Houses of the Dead: Book Three
Copyright © 2020 Leah Cutter
All rights reserved
Published by Knotted Road Press
www.KnottedRoadPress.com

ISBN: 978-1-64470-191-1

Cover Art:

ID 26087942 © Dusan Kostic | Dreamstime.com

Cover and interior design copyright © 2020 Knotted Road Press
http://www.KnottedRoadPress.com

Reviews
It's true. Reviews help me sell more books. If you've enjoyed this story, please consider leaving a review of it on your favorite site.

Come someplace new...
Are you a traveler? Do you enjoy exploring strange new worlds, new cultures, new people?

Journey into the various lands envisioned by Leah Cutter.

Sign up for my newsletter and I'll start you on your travels with a free copy of my book, *The Island Sampler*.

http://www.LeahCutter.com/newsletter/

Also by Leah R Cutter

Forgotten Gods

A Wind Blown Torment

A Stone Strewn Clash

A Sea Washed Victory

Tanish Empire Trilogy

The Glass Magician

The Desert Heart

The Ghost Dog

The Cassie Stories

Poisoned Pearls

Tainted Waters

Spoiled Harvest

Bloodied Ice

The Witch's Progress

Circle of Air

Circle of Water

Circle of Fire

Circle of Earth

Seattle Trolls

The Changeling Troll

The Princess Troll

Chapter One
HOUSE OF CRYSTAL

IT HAD ONLY BEEN a few days since Akalina had been in the palace. It hadn't even taken her a full week to travel up to Sitre's Hold with her sister Befery, to convince Yimifut to take on the mantle of LandHolder.

But everything felt different, now. It was as though the palace had shrunk while she'd been gone.

Or maybe she'd just grown bigger. Not in height, but on the inside. Older. Wiser. More settled into her skin. Though she was still infertile—that cold emptiness still lay buried deep inside of her.

She was sadder, too. So many ghosts had sacrificed their existence to stop Darikuto.

Yimifut and the others were only going to be here in Nyati overnight. In the morning, they were being thrown by Yimifut all the way across the lands of the House of Gold, and into battle with the House of Cobalt. Every Holder was sending their warriors along, as well as farmers and others who had no training. While Yimifut would carry most of the people, everyone who had even a smidgen of magic was being asked to help.

Unnir, the LandHolder for the House of Gold, was under attack. And losing, according to Yimifut.

Akalina didn't really have a lot to do until they left in the morning. She'd spent an incredibly awkward hour with her parents who still didn't understand a single thing about her or what she was doing, leaving as quickly as she could before she ended up yelling at them, saying things she might not regret later.

She found herself wandering out of her rooms, into the more public areas, then down the hallway to the ghost court.

A young boy sat alone in the cold, empty room. The long table set up for the ghosts' feasts had a single silver bowl sitting in the center of it. The sweet smell of the smoking incense lingered in the air, masking the smell of dust and ash. No ghosts sat in any of the two-dozen carved wooden chairs. Akalina couldn't even hear their whispering in the corners.

It appeared that the ghosts had abandoned their own court. Surely they hadn't all accompanied her to the battle?

The long windows across the wall opposite the door were all shut, the frosted glass hiding the shadowed stone courtyard beyond. The room itself was unadorned by any artwork or carvings: the ghosts didn't need or want such things, so the walls were bare as a crypt. A huge hearth made for heated rocks stood at one end of the room, not empty but cold. Just a single candelabra was lit on the table, leaving the corners of the room in shadows.

"Hello," the boy said, standing abruptly. "I'm Pabi."

Akalina nodded her greeting, remembering the boy. He was a cousin of sorts, related to her uncle through marriage. She'd met him once or twice, at a feast or festival, but she hadn't really paid that much attention to him, as he was probably only twelve at this point, and she was seventeen, going on thirty, or at least that was how she felt that night.

Pabi wore the typical ghost court garb: a long-sleeved

white shirt overlaid with spiderweb lace that buttoned tightly around his neck and covered his hands to his fingertips, along with a pair of very plain black trousers. His black hair needed cutting, as it flowed past his shoulders and his bangs hung down over his eyes. Powder had been applied to his face, to make his pale skin whiter.

"I'm Akalina," she said when she realized he didn't know her either.

"Oh, oh!" he said, his dark brown eyes widening. "Are you here to bring all the ghosts back?"

"What do you mean?" Akalina said. True, the ghosts did follow her everywhere, it seemed. The room had been empty of their presence when she'd first stepped in, but she could now hear their sibilant whispering. She still couldn't see them, even in the dark corners.

Pabi looked at the ground for a moment, ashamed. "Well, they, they said that the reason we don't have ghosts any more is because you took them all."

Akalina snorted in derision. "By *they* you mean Menhaptu, right?"

The boy nodded, looking apprehensive. "I didn't think that you would take them. I mean, how could anyone take our ghosts? I figured they just probably liked you better than him."

Pabi's eyes grew wide and his hands flew to his mouth, covering it, as if he could hide the words he'd just said. "Don't tell him I said that!" he pleaded.

"I won't," Akalina assured the boy with a grin. She wasn't about to get Pabi in trouble with the stupid priest, since she held a very low opinion of the man herself.

Movement caught her eye. A white ghostly figure had just come through the wall, between the windows. The top of the ghost was made out of a well-defined white mist, from his head down to his waist. Below the waist, he

3

appeared to have no legs and just floated on a cloud. He was an older man, dressed in old-fashioned court finery. He had a thin face and a sharp chin and looked around with displeasure.

Based on how white the figure was, Akalina knew it was one of the younger ghosts. The older the ghost, the darker their appearance.

It made sense, actually, that only the younger ghosts were here now, as many of the older, more powerful ghosts had sacrificed themselves to stop Darikuto and his warriors, to save the land for Yimifut.

Would they accompany her to the next battle? Travel all the way across the House of Gold lands? Or would she call the ghosts in that land to her?

She didn't know. She didn't think the ghosts knew, either.

But just in case, they needed their sustenance, as it were.

"We need to set out more incense for them," Akalina directed Pabi. "A grand feast, before the ghosts join us in battle tomorrow."

The boy nodded solemnly, though it was obvious he had no idea why she was making him do it.

Akalina went to the cupboard that took up the wall opposite the cold hearth. Fine silver bowls already filled with resin and incense waited there. Delicate round fans that resembled clam shells took up an entire shelf. On the side table stood three elegant candelabras, with tall beeswax candles.

Akalina started handing out implements to the boy, who rushed to set them on the table. "Careful, slowly!" Akalina admonished.

The boy nodded and suddenly started moving with a slow, steady grace.

While sharp winds wouldn't disrupt the ghosts, they still didn't like breezes ruffling their wavery edges. All the attendants to the court of the ghosts were trained to move smoothly and slowly, not causing any errant air currents.

As Pabi set the table, more ghosts came filing in. Akalina was startled to realize that many of the ghosts seated at the table weren't part of the regular court. They wore plain clothes, even the aprons of guildmembers.

Pabi, too, realized that these weren't his usual customers at the ghost feast. He raised his eyebrows, questioning their appearance.

Akalina shrugged. It made her heart ache to think about the ghosts who'd died, who were now really dead, who'd sacrificed themselves for the House of Crystal.

Whatever it takes.

Even if that meant allowing commoners in among the court royals.

All of the two-dozen chairs were quickly filled with ghostly figures, sucking up the "feast" of smoke from the incense. They whispered quietly amongst themselves, not bothering to talk with either Akalina or Pabi. More ghosts waited their turn quietly in the corner. Akalina quickly set the rocks in the hearth to glow with a golden light and warmth.

As soon as the first set of ghosts departed, the chairs were filled again. Mostly commoners now, just a couple of figures from the old court. All younger ghosts still, bright white and well-defined.

It took will to remain a ghost, to not pass into the underworld. In addition to being whiter, the newer ghosts also tended to be better defined, as their will was still young and stronger.

Akalina and Pabi moved silently and smoothly, like ghosts themselves, refilling incense bowls, replacing candles, adding more fans if a ghost took one with them.

The third set of ghosts was again, mostly younger ghosts

and commoners. It was only after they'd left that the older ghosts came in. Akalina recognized some of them, like Mehete, who'd been a famous sculptor in his time. These ghosts moved more slowly than the others. Their presence had a weight to it, reminding Akalina of still pools on the edges of a flowing stream.

The ghosts settled in around the table, feasting silently. Akalina and Pabi stood at the edge of the room, watching them, ready to come forward and refill any of the incense holders.

As no other ghosts waited in the corners or near the hearth, Akalina figured this was the final group. Pabi couldn't hide a jaw-splitting yawn. He was obviously exhausted.

Akalina had no idea what time it was, but she knew that it was late. Pabi had probably been just about to go to bed.

"Go," she told him quietly. "You don't need to stay. I'll take care of this group."

Pabi tried to argue, but found himself yawning again. "Are you sure?" he asked shaking his head, as if trying to deny how tired he was.

"I am," Akalina said, still feeling years older than seventeen. "Go."

"Will there be any ghosts for me to tend to in the morning?" Pabi said, looking seriously at her.

"I don't know," Akalina said. "Should I ask one to stay?"

He shrugged. "It would be nice to have something to actually do. So I feel as though I'm doing my duty."

"I'll see if I can get one or more to stay," Akalina promised him.

With another stifled yawn, Pabi wandered off.

As she'd expected, as soon as the boy had left, one of the ghosts beckoned Akalina closer to the table.

Akalina didn't recognize the woman. The ghost wore a heavy apron over her top, so Akalina assumed she was in a guild, possibly even a GuildHolder. She wore her hair in short curls, her cheeks were chubby and she had a large, squishy nose that had obviously been broken and never healed straight.

"I am Retisi," she said in a stronger voice than most ghosts had. It sounded more like someone speaking quietly than a whisper. "We go with you tomorrow. As many as who can, all the way through the foreign lands."

"Thank you," Akalina said, knowing that it was likely to be a death sentence for many of them. "How can I help?"

"Burn incense for us, every night," Retisi said. "And every morning as well. We will fight, beside the living, for the first time ever."

"What are we facing?" Akalina asked. She'd heard that Kinaki had been taken over by a demon, and that other demons from the underworld now walked the lands of the living.

"Corruption," Retisi said. The other ghosts around the table sighed, as if they were facing a heavy task. "You must stay pure, no matter what."

Akalina knew that Retisi wasn't just talking about the demons. Akalina was a virgin, and must remain so. "For the rest of my life?" she said, not really wanting to know, but feeling compelled to ask.

"Maybe," Retisi said. "Maybe not. That future is too difficult for even us to see."

Akalina nodded, then withdrew back to the side as the ghosts finished their feast.

She'd felt so alone here, cut off from her family and all of the living. Almost like a ghost herself.

Seemed that might be her fate in life.

Chapter Two
HOUSE OF COBALT

❦

Kinaki paced in front of his tent, growling with satisfaction as warriors continued to be belched out of the land on a nearby hill.

Soon, they would attack Unnir's puny forces in a single, massive wave.

Just as his army had swelled, Kinaki also felt swollen and bloated, like a man who'd sat down at a fine repast and hadn't known when to stop eating.

Or like a tick who'd drunk too much blood.

He knew that his body had changed in the aftermath of his fight with Wanho. Physically, he was taller, towering over all his WarHolders and CollierHolders. Perhaps some of his warriors now came up to the middle of his chest. None reached his shoulders. He was also more massive. It wasn't all muscle, though he could now, with a single thought, change the corpulent fat into something much harder.

The fat and weight settled him, pounding his massive feet into the ground. He felt his senses completely attuned to the land. The ashes he tasted were better than the finest wine. The corruption he felt pulsing through his veins was more exciting than any woman. The call of the warriors as they tumbled out of the hill, hailing their comrades, was the sweetest music he'd ever heard.

While Wanho had hoped that the battle with Kinaki in the underworld would end up with the demon more in control, possibly even with Kinaki's consciousness shuffled off to one side, the opposite had occurred. They were more firmly twined around each other than ever.

Part of Kinaki's new weight was how he wore the demon's body. Wanho had been like a great snake wrapped around Kinaki's torso. Now, though, the demon had moved under his skin. Kinaki no longer felt the coils shifting, no longer felt Wanho's whispered words weighing down his soul.

They were still separate, but less so than they had been. More a single creature—a newly forged entity.

Wanho had learned how Kinaki had rescued his children, getting a message through to Sunli, the priest. As part of their negotiations, Kinaki agreed to stop doing the warrior exercises. Kinaki had readily agreed, as he was no longer certain that they would put the demon to sleep.

In addition, Kinaki had learned that Wanho had been trying to get rid of him. It was part of why they were bound so closely together, now.

The battle between them hadn't taken long. Wanho had underestimated Kinaki's will, how the LandHolder had drawn not just on the power of his own land, but also the bedrock underneath, that supported all of the houses.

It was how Kinaki planned on taking over all of the lands.

It was more difficult to feel that bedrock now, up here, in the land of the living. He suspected that the corruptions of the House of Cobalt made it more difficult as well.

But he was determined to figure out how to do it.

He'd had a taste of pure power. He wanted more.

Or so he told himself.

He ignored the part of him that was buried so deep that he could rarely find it, the part that was still human, who mourned his children turning against him as well as how the land had changed.

That part was unimportant in the grand scheme of things.

Kinaki wasn't sure if it was he who had that sentiment, or Wanho. It was an academic question at best.

He and the demon were joined together, now and forever, unless the gods sundered them apart one day.

Kinaki planned on ruling forever. Wanho could support their physical form, and Kinaki would always be able to taste the bedrock of the land.

It was just a matter of time before Kinaki took that next step forward, his warriors attacking Unnir's forces, and he took the lands of the House of Gold for himself.

Chapter Three

HOUSE OF GOLD

❧

UNNIR'S HEAD felt as though the pain would split it in two if she bent over too quickly. Her mouth was dry from arguing with her VeinHolders all night, plotting and planning how to survive the next day, when Kinaki's much greater forces attacked. She'd forced down a bit of bread and some cheese while they'd planned, but her stomach wouldn't tolerate much, feeling as though knots upon knots were tightening there.

Help was coming. Yimifut, the new LandHolder for the House of Crystal, as well as Darikuto, were on their way.

But they wouldn't arrive until the next night. Though they'd bring more warriors, the two LandHolders would be exhausted from moving so many people such a great distance.

The House of Gold just needed to survive until then.

Unnir wasn't certain they could. Particularly since she and Vide had already divided her forces, planning on surprising and capturing some of Kinaki's warriors who'd snuck across the edges of her border.

She needed help, and not just from the other LandHolders.

Despite her exhaustion, Unnir left the meeting with her VeinHolders and marched over to Vide's tent.

A guard stood outside the tent flap. She looked at Unnir, opened her mouth, then shut it again firmly.

Whatever the warrior had wanted to warn Unnir about hadn't seemed important in the face of Unnir's great need.

Instead, the guard flipped back the tent flap and gestured for Unnir to enter.

The tent smelled like a brewery. Bottles were stacked up on the table, along the edges of the tent, and strewn across the floor. It looked as though Vide had drunk an entire Vein's worth of wine since Emil had been killed.

Normally, books, maps, and notes covered the table, the boxes alongside of it, as well as the chairs. It took Unnir a moment to spy them all jumbled together in a heap on one side. It reminded her of her little boy, after being told to clean his room, who'd jumbled everything together to one side hoping that would be good enough.

Dirt caked the fine rug that covered the middle of the tent. Honestly, that surprised Unnir most of all. Vide was fastidious when it came to cleaning.

Unnir stepped forward and with a wave of her hand, cleaned the rug and sent all the bottles into neat stacks by the side of the tent flap.

Only then did she finally catch a glimpse of Vide. He was under a pile of blankets on his cot, sleeping like the dead. His already pale face was much whiter, as if the life had been bleached out of him. His black hair looked matted.

As Unnir drew closer, a sour smell overwhelmed the smell of the spilled wine. Vide had vomited up whatever he'd eaten. Then kept drinking. And had vomited again.

Unnir used her magic to empty the bedpan of its foul

contents. She didn't touch Vide, though. Instead, she cleared one of the chairs and sat next to his cot.

She watched him sleep for a few moments, unsure of how to wake him, when he suddenly said, "You know, it's kind of creepy, you just sitting there and staring at me as if I'm going to suddenly sprout feathers or something."

"How long have you been awake?" Unnir asked.

"Long enough to know you did a bit of cleaning. Thank you," Vide said.

He opened his eyes, turning his head, and squinted at Unnir. "You look like shit," he commented.

"Feel like it," she said. "Kinaki will attack in a few hours with a force that is twice the size it was yesterday. No one will get here to help until tomorrow evening."

Unnir felt even more tired after saying the words aloud, as if the weight of what was coming had also doubled.

After a few long moments, Vide finally asked, "So? What do you expect me to do about it?"

Stung, Unnir replied, "We all promised to put aside our differences while the war played out."

"That was before *you* lost Emil," Vide said. His pale eyes sparked to life. "There is no bargain that I will hold, now. Not without…without him…by my side."

"I'm sorry," Unnir said automatically. Then she paused, and added, "You know? Scratch that. I'm *not* sorry that Emil died. He died doing his duty to the land as well as to his LandHolder. Which is *me* in case you hadn't noticed."

Vide's gray eyes narrowed. "And?" he asked archly.

"You want to mourn the loss of your brother properly. I understand that," Unnir said. "But we have no time. The entire world will end come dawn if we don't do something about it."

"So?" Vide said. He turned his head and looked back up at the ceiling of the tent. "Let it die."

Unnir stood. The room spun and the edges darkened. She really, *really* needed to rest for a short bit before the sun rose. "You know what? Emil would be ashamed of you. He'd grown. Changed. Become a leader. You? Still can't see beyond your own selfish nose. People have died already. Good warriors. So many more are going to die tomorrow as well. Other people's brothers. Or husbands. Or friends. You can either help stem that onslaught. Or you can just go back to Haravik with your tail between your legs. But if you go back, you better start making sacrifices to the gods now, pray with all your might that we succeed. Or you will get your wish. And the world will die."

Unnir turned and left the tent, her anger carrying her at least a little way, out of the still stinking tent and into the cool evening air.

Gods *damn* her selfish cousin. She really could use his help right now. Could really use his sneaky ways and plots to stop Kinaki as well as survive the next couple of days.

The world was set against her, though.

Unnir made it back to her tent then collapsed into her own cot. All the terrible words, the awful, upcoming deeds, piled up on top of her, holding her down like a corpse weighed down with rocks.

She reached deep into the land, *her* land, delved down into the good solid soil, feeling the peace that was always there, the bounty of the harvest, the richness of the gold in the mines. She wasn't sure if she slept or just rested there, in the bosom of her true soul.

When the call came she rose and prepared herself as well as she could.

The day was going to be hell. She had to live with the fact that she'd done everything she could.

And it was never going to be enough.

THE SLAUGHTER STARTED AT DAWN.

Unnir saw Kinaki's forces sweeping across the battlefield as a dark wave, obliterating everything in its path.

Her warriors crumbled, overwhelmed. They had discipline. They fought well.

And they died.

The ones who'd stepped beyond the curtain that still protected the border understood that their lives were forfeit. Chances were, none of them would survive, except in songs and legends told about that day.

They still fought on, desperate to hold on to their side for even a short while. An hour. Maybe more.

Unnir didn't time it, but she knew that they might have held out for perhaps an hour and a half.

No longer.

Then the demons were pounding on the border. The tall, shimmering golden curtain wavered as they slashed at it with their weapons and their claws.

Unnir sat cross-legged on the ground on a nearby hill, all her focus on maintaining the line. She breathed in the hot winds on the far side of the curtain, felt the foulness of the land over there. Ashes smeared across her skin. The sound of bones being smashed underfoot filled her ears. Her stomach heaved at the stench of the rot and gore.

She stayed still, pouring all the magic she could tap into the border line. That curtain had to hold, had to keep the enemy out. Maybe she could save them all—maintain it until evening, when the other LandHolders would arrive.

"LandHolder!" came a desperate cry.

Unnir tried to split her focus, to see the world around her as well as maintain the border.

She knew she was doomed to fail.

"The border's been breached! We have to be away! Now!"

Torja's face was white with ash, her mouth red with blood.

Or maybe that was just Unnir's impression of the head priestess.

"The warriors you allowed in through the curtain. The plan that you and Vide came up with, to trap them here. They're attacking on this side, right now!" Torja said.

Was that Vide just beyond her? Possibly.

Unnir blinked, and turned her gaze back toward the curtain that still held Kinaki's forces back.

But now, she felt streams of corruption that flowed under the curtain, tethered beyond her camp, held there by the demons she'd allowed into her lands already.

They were already lost. She just hadn't realized it yet.

She nodded and closed her eyes, reaching deep into the land, pulling up every bit of magic that she could find.

Then she flung the entire camp two miles north, with herself in the center of it. Reassembled the border curtain. It was stronger here, as it was fresh and new.

She didn't know how long it would stand, before she'd have to retreat again.

It would take Kinaki's demons a while to cross the distance. There were plenty of boobytraps to take care of some of them, so they wouldn't arrive in strength for another hour. Maybe two.

Then, hopefully, she'd be able to hold them here.

Otherwise, she'd have to keep retreating. Again, and again. Until all that was left was Haravik, the capital itself, where she intended to make her final stand.

The others would arrive well before then.

And they'd help her defeat Kinaki.

Right?

Chapter Four
HOUSE OF PEARL

❧

DARIKUTO RESENTED the forced march across the flat plains of the lands of the House of Gold. The sun beat down on all of them, draining their strength. Though he had fewer warriors than he'd started out with—damn those warriors from the House of Crystal—they were still an awful burden to carry.

There were no breaks, not really, not for him. They didn't stop to eat. The warriors marched on, nibbling on hardtack or jerky, sipping stale, warm water from canteens. Darikuto was reduced to doing the same, his mouth dry and full of salt.

Sure, he might have been able to draw up a bottle of wine, conjure it from one of the packs left behind. But he needed to conserve all his strength for the move they were making.

He thought about The New Plan when he could. However, under the duress of moving so many warriors so many miles, he couldn't get any good planning or scenario gaming going. Still, he pondered when he could, remembering that girl, the one who could command the ghosts. As well as the solid feel of bedrock, that lay far beneath all the lands.

It was so obvious, that core. Why had none of the books he'd read speak of that solid reality? Or had the others never felt it?

Except, there was that one. That talked of the river of rock flowing beneath the soil. Darikuto had discounted it as poetic license.

Had it been? He must find that book again.

A loud noise behind him snapped his attention back to the dusty, hot road and the grumbling warriors all around him. He glanced back, but saw no one trying to get his attention or impeding on his space.

Gods damn it! He wanted some time to think. To plan. To draw up perfect scenarios and then think of ways to defeat them.

Chuyoko was a warrior. She was meant for action.

Darikuto could put plans into motion, but he needed that plan first!

With a sigh, Darikuto reached around him, gathering up his proud warriors, flinging them further down the road.

Up ahead, he sensed the darkness that held the lands of the House of Cobalt. It had grown worse, so much worse, in the short time since he'd last been there.

For a moment, Darikuto knew doubt.

The first Plan had succeeded too well.

Except—there was something sweetly familiar about those clouds ahead. He knew he could grow to love them. These lands could stay infected, as long as the House of Pearl remained pure, her waters uncorrupted.

Would it be possible to have both? To revel in the ashes and pure power of the other lands, while keeping his own untainted?

It was just another aspect of The New Plan that he'd have to consider, and then put into place when the time arose.

"Yes?" Darikuto snapped at the person who approached him. It had been a long hard day of travel. They still hadn't reached the border. He didn't want to admit that they might not reach it before midnight.

Yimifut had gotten there ahead of him. How? The pipsqueak was barely a man, let alone a LandHolder. Yes, of course he'd been crossing his own land. Still, he shouldn't have had the strength or ability.

Darikuto had still called a break, so that the warriors could eat an evening meal and prepare to be thrown directly into battle, if need be.

He sat alone, the early evening sunlight pouring out across the land, stifling the air. How could anyone love such a flat place? It boggled the mind. There were no trees, no woods, no breaks in the monotonous landscape.

Yet, people chose to live here.

The meal had been cold but substantial, all the wine, flat bread, and hard cheese that he could eat. No one had the time to conjure anything more fancy.

Now, Darikuto was just breathing in the peace of the approaching evening when someone had the audacity to bother him.

"Yes?" he asked again, looking around.

Chuyoko stood there. The tiny woman's expression was bland, as if afraid to show any emotion. She wore her lightest armor, just leathers, really. The sword at her back was almost as big as she was. However, Darikuto knew that she could handle it better one-handed when she was exhausted than most hulks could at the start of a day with both hands.

"You asked me to come and see you before the last big push," she reminded him.

Darikuto tried to pull his thoughts together. "Yes," he said slowly. "You need to keep a reserve of warriors. A fall back. In case we get overwhelmed and need to retreat."

Chuyoko narrowed her eyes at him. "Are you not expecting us to win?"

Darikuto could hear the disdain in her voice. "No, not that. Not at all." He sighed. He was too tired to have to explain every little thing to people all the time. But Chuyoko had to understand the possibilities.

"There may come a point when it's more advantageous for us to retreat than to keep pushing forward. For Unnir to lose more of her land."

"I see," Chuyoko said, though she obviously didn't.

Darikuto sighed again. Chuyoko was a warrior—one of the best in all the lands. But she was a sword, who didn't understand that sometimes, an arrow or even a dart was sometimes more effective.

"I will tell you when the time comes," Darikuto said, dismissing her.

Chuyoko looked as though she wanted to argue, then she bowed her head and marched back to the other PearlHolders.

They wouldn't want to retreat, not in the heat of battle. But it might be necessary to lose a little, in order for Darikuto to come riding in at the end, defeating Kinaki after Unnir had already been lost.

Then, it would just be Darikuto and Yimifut who wrestled for control of all the lands everywhere.

This time, Darikuto would be victorious.

He was sure of it.

Chapter Five
HOUSE OF CRYSTAL

AKALINA WASN'T sure what to expect, traveling all the way across the House of Gold lands to the far border. She'd traveled with Ibitsima before, where every step they took moved them many steps aross the land. It had been a weird way to travel, but it wasn't that disturbing. It meant things passed by more quickly, in somewhat of a jerky fashion.

Traveling with Yimifut had been different. There was the feeling of moving too fast. Yimifut seemed to *fling* them, so that one step was worth more than a mile. Akalina would blink, and everything would have changed. The small hill she'd been focused on would be gone, now standing far behind her, and there would be a depression in the field instead.

It was unsettling, for her feet to never be fully connected to the ground. The Land was all around her, she could feel it, but she couldn't touch it, not really.

They reached the border just after sunset. The great golden curtain that demarcated the end of the House of Gold was a quite a sight. It stretched up as far as the eye could see, and from horizon to horizon. It undulated slightly, as if stroked by a faint breeze that Akalina couldn't see.

"It's in the wrong place," Yimifut said after a few moments.

Akalina just looked at him, uncertain what he meant.

"The old border was several miles south of here. Unnir has had to retreat. More than once," he said.

Akalina thought of Yimifut as generally deliberate. He wasn't one to move quickly over, well, just about anything.

But now, even his words were coming out slowly.

How much had the march cost her LandHolder?

Befery came bustling up. She thrust a hunk of bread at Yimifut. "Eat," she said sternly. Then she handed Akalina a smaller piece. "You, too." She glared at them both.

Yimifut nodded and took a small bite, followed by a much bigger one. "And here's some meat," Befery said, handing him a hunk from a smoked ham. She glanced at Akalina and gave a small shrug, before handing the LandHolder a flagon of water.

Akalina understood that she was to get herself the rest, that Befery was there to make sure that Yimifut ate and was taken care of.

She was fiercely glad that her sister was there, that she understood what the LandHolder needed, better than he understood himself.

Even if that meant that she was on her own. As always.

While Akalina was finding herself food, guards from Unnir's camp came up cautiously, verifying that they were, indeed, there to help.

A messenger came to find Akalina as she stood munching on a rind of cheese. She was dressed in a gray tunic with a badge in the center made out of a multitude of braided green ribbons.

Akalina had never seen such a badge before, but she

assumed that it identified the messenger as coming from the House of Gold.

"You are asked to attend the meeting of the LandHolders," the messenger said formally.

Akalina gulped. Since she'd been left behind by Ibitsima, Akalina had assumed that she wouldn't really have dealings with the LandHolders again. Yimifut didn't need her. Not really.

At her nod, the messenger turned sharply and walked away a few feet. Then she stopped and turned back, making sure that Akalina was following.

Wiping her hands on her travel-stained trousers, Akalina did what was expected of her and hurried after the messenger, though she felt like dragging her heels, unsure of what doom she was heading toward.

AKALINA HADN'T EXPECTED the LandHolders would be meeting outside. She'd expected them to be in a tent, at the very least. But they stood together on the crest of a slight hill, looking down into the bowl. Others stood there with them— Akalina thought she recognized Vide, Unnir's cousin, as well as Shimokoro, the head priest of the Temple of Truth for the House of Pearl.

Lights danced around the group, unobtrusive but glowing brightly enough that everyone could see each other. Yimifut still looked exhausted, his pale skin drained of color. Darikuto's dark skin hid his fatigue better, but Akalina had the sense that he, too, was barely keeping himself upright.

Unnir appeared to be in the worst shape of all of them, her cheeks sunken, as if she'd lost weight suddenly. Her eyes looked haunted and burned with a dark fire.

"Thank you for attending us," Unnir said, greeting

Akalina. "Yimifut says that you have a special ability that you would like to show us."

It took Akalina a moment to figure out what she meant. "Oh. You mean the ghosts," she said.

"Yes. Exactly," Darikuto said. He seemed to have suddenly awoken.

Akalina didn't like the way he looked at her, as if he were trying to determine just how to slice her meat from her bones.

"I can try," Akalina said. "I need some incense, and some candles."

Unnir nodded and a table was conjured a few feet away. A silver brazier filled with incense was already lit, smoking sweetly, along with four candles on either end.

Akalina stepped up to the table, unsure of what to do next. She thought for a moment, before she used a bit of her own magic to call up the slightest breeze, sending thin trails of the smoke from the incense into the night.

Then Akalina reached down with her landsense. She felt the sharp edge of the border of the House of Gold, as if a knife had been sliced along the ground, opening a chasm between the two lands.

She shied away from that direction, turning her attention north, toward her own home. She knew it was just her imagination, but she would swear that she felt cool mountain winds blowing toward her.

How was she to call the ghosts? They'd come with her to the last battle, against Darikuto. She just had to direct them.

This time, she had to find them.

Or, perhaps, act as a beacon so that they could find her.

Akalina put her hands over her womb, that spot that Rosahaptu had killed, deep within her, making her sterile. The cold she always felt was there, just under her skin, filling her palms with the cool moonlight of the ghosts.

She couldn't pull that spot out of her. No one could heal her. The ghosts had marked her as different, as other.

So that she could be alone, as always.

And more like them.

Akalina pushed her breath into that terrible spot, then breathed out that cold. She felt it gathering around her, like the mist of the ghosts. The lights from the gathering grew dim as the fog grew.

At first, the mists were indistinct. Slowly, the fog coalesced into the shapes of ghosts, torsos and heads floating around her.

She recognized some of the ghosts from the House of Crystal, who appeared to have made the long journey here with her. But they only made up about a third of the beings she could see. The rest were strangers to her, dressed in the long, formal robes of the House of Gold.

One of the local ghosts stepped up to her. He was a young ghost, bright white and well defined, with a proud mien. Akalina would have bet that when he'd been alive, he'd had cruel eyes.

"I am Yudur," he announced.

From the gasps behind her, Akalina guessed that he was very recently dead, that there were those who had known him when he'd been alive. She vaguely recognized the name —wait. Was this the former LandHolder? Who'd been in charge of the House of Gold before Unnir?

"I know how to beat this demon," he continued, as if no one had replied. Then he paused. He looked over Akalina's shoulder, directly at Unnir. "If you would have my help, LandHolder."

Akalina knew that there had been bad blood between the two of them. She knew that someone like Yudur would never just apologize for his behavior.

Asking to be allowed to help, instead of insisting, was probably the best he could do.

Akalina glanced over her shoulder at Unnir. Despite the woman's exhaustion, she suddenly looked relieved.

"Thank you, Uncle," Unnir said clearly. "Your help would be much appreciated."

Yudur nodded. "We will attack come dawn," he said. Then he paused and shot a hard look directly at Akalina. "You know the cost," he warned.

Then Yudur, and the army of ghosts that had gathered, suddenly disappeared.

Akalina gulped when she turned around to face the LandHolders.

The cost would be not just a reduction in the amount of foretelling from the priests of the Temple of Truth. No, it would also mean that the lands of the House of Gold would contain less magic.

Akalina looked at Yimifut, who nodded at her. At least he understood.

Whatever it took.

Chapter Six
HOUSE OF COBALT

WANHO SHIFTED UNCOMFORTABLY as he dozed, deep inside Kinaki's body.

The epic battle that the demon had planned with the living LandHolder had not gone as he'd expected. He had assumed that naked and weak, Kinaki would be easily overwhelmed when brought to the underworld.

That at the end, Kinaki would be banished to a small corner of his own mind, and Wanho would be in charge.

That the battle had ended in a draw, and that they'd had to negotiate with each other still left a bad taste in Wanho's mouth, as if fresh water had been poured into it. Or wine, sweetened with pure honey, instead of water swirling with ashes or wine soured to vinegar.

They'd merged at a deeper level than Wanho had known was possible. Still, he was a separate creature, more so than Kinaki. He had more will when it came to moving their shared, magnificent, corpulent body around.

Plus, Kinaki had agreed to stop practicing his warrior training, stop sending Wanho into a daze where he was no longer fully conscious.

While Wanho had *not* agreed to stop seeking how to end their relationship.

It was still only a matter of time before he'd be the one fully in charge.

And if he were killed? It wouldn't really matter. He'd just go back to being a demon in the underworld. Sure, when the body of the living most demons died once the body of the living they'd been inhabiting had died. But not all demons. The stronger ones survived.

All right, so maybe it was only one or two.

Wanho was willing to bet on those odds. He'd survive, no matter what.

Despite their merging, Kinaki's body still needed sleep. Wanho didn't sleep, not like the living did. He did rest, albeit not peacefully. But there wasn't much he could do. Kinaki had to sleep.

Wanho shifted again. The scent of the night had changed. It would be dawn soon. There were no stupid birds to waken him—that was for the living.

No, there would be battle soon, more blood and carnage to feast on. Today, they would drive their enemy back all the way to her puny city. Once their enemy was trapped there, Wanho was certain he could open up another eruption of warriors, deep inside the walls of the city.

Unnir would die. The magic she held would seep back into the land, ready for the taking, as there would be no heir. The land wouldn't choose another, not when it was corrupted as it was.

Wanho planned to sup on all that power, draw it deep within himself.

He didn't intend to share it.

It wouldn't give him the strength to rid himself of Kinaki. Not yet.

But perhaps after they defeated the House of Crystal, that accumulated power would be enough to free him.

Wanho caused the body to take another deep breath, reveling in the ash that still flavored the air.

Soon.

❀

THOUGH KINAKI SEEMED dismayed at the way that Unnir's forces had swelled overnight, joined by the House of Crystal as well as the House of Pearl, Wanho continued to have no doubt that Cobalt's forces were superior.

More of the living poured out from behind that soiled curtain that marked the newest border, that place where Unnir had been forced to retreat to.

Wanho roared with pleasure as the first wave of his warriors attacked. They were fighting on flat fields now. The boots of his warriors churned the ground into mud, killing anything that tried to grow there. The clang of sword and shield beat like a pulsing heart. Red blood poured out, the best sacrifice Wanho could wish for. Clouds of insects gathered above the field, gnats, flies, and other pests waiting their due.

The battle continued. Wanho and Kinaki prepared to join their WarHolders, to slaughter all those before them. None dared face their gigantic being. The sword they wielded swept bodies to the side, sending them flying through the air, like rake-tossed leaves.

As soon as Wanho stepped onto the battlefield, they felt the difference.

Something wasn't right with the land. The border between where the fighting was fiercest and where the warrior's tents had been set up, where Wanho had spent the morning, was obvious.

Though this had been House of Gold land until just the day before, Unnir had released all claim to it. Kinaki had claimed it as his own almost immediately.

If a LandHolder didn't take hold of freed land, it would grow wild. With a mind of its own, it might or might not tolerate the living.

The ground beneath Wanho's feet was still unclaimed.

How could that be?

Kinaki forced their shared body to stop. He couldn't go forward, couldn't fight, not with land just waiting for the taking all around him.

No! Wanho tried to shout.

Kinaki, the LandHolder, was able to override the demon.

This was *Land.*

All of their shared attention dove deep under the ground, their landsense spreading out in an attempt to find the borders of this piece of earth with no claim to it.

The edges seemed soft, as though cotton batting was wrapped across the border. Even as Kinaki pushed into it, it gave way, the land demanding *more.*

Helpless, Wanho felt Kinaki reach through him to the demons still fighting the living somewhere up above them.

Wanho had occasionally pushed power out to individuals fighting, to help the army conquer their enemies.

Now, Kinaki used that line to tug that power back, to transfer it into this greedy maw of land that refused to succumb to his will.

It's a trap, Wanho tried to convey as more and more magic was channeled into the very earth, Kinaki drawing it from all around him.

The screams of the warriors finally pierced Kinaki's focus.

"What is it?" he asked, his attention returning to the battlefield.

Wanho blinked their eyes, unable to process what he was seeing.

It was as if the golden curtain had started smoking. Billows of mist rolled out from it, streams of fog that obscured his view.

Somehow, the ghosts of the land had been called into action. They sucked at all the power that Kinaki had dumped into the ground, trying to reclaim the untamed land.

Then used it against his demon warriors.

Ghosts were the dead who remained in the land of the living. They had no power to affect the living.

The warriors who made up Wanho's WarHolders weren't necessarily completely living. Most of them either bore demons or had a demon mark, showing that the body bore both a soul of the living and a demon.

The ghosts greedily sucked the power out of them as well when they tried to engage.

Roaring with displeasure, Wanho directed their shared body forward. They swept their great sword from side to side, tossing the enemy warriors away.

The ghosts dared not attack them straight on. Instead, they parted like a curtain, flowing around and behind Wanho.

Surrounding him.

Wanho did *not* want to retreat, damn it! They had Unnir on the run. The army shouldn't have rested that night, but pushed forward, even though Wanho understood that wouldn't have been possible.

The living needed to rest.

Wanho's warriors could rest when they were dead.

Still, Wanho felt the insidious way the ghosts started to suck at the power of the LandHolder. They still used Kinaki's connection to the land to slip in under his armor, to place their careful darts, to sip at the LandHolder's mighty strength.

No! screamed Wanho as Kinaki took a step backwards.

Then another step.

The rest of the warriors sensed the change on the field, even without their WarHolders or CollierHolders saying a word.

As one, all of Kinaki's warriors began to pull back.

Unnir's combined forces surged forward, eager for the kill.

The screams of demons filled the air, unleashing their agony to the clouds.

Kinaki continued to slowly move backwards, retreating step by step.

And Wanho suddenly understood the meaning of *nightmare*, as he saw the golden curtain of the border begin to inch forward.

Chapter Seven
HOUSE OF GOLD

THE COOL FEELING of the ghosts surrounding Chaotu made him distinctly uneasy. It was as if spiders crawled over his flesh, raising goosepimples and sending constant shivers down his spine.

It was good.

It reminded him that he was alive, and that he had a job to fulfill.

No matter what it cost.

Chaotu saw the looks the other warriors gave him after Emil had sacrificed himself to save him. One of the VeinHolders had even yelled at him for not paying attention to his surroundings, for rushing forward and not seeing the obvious trap.

Chaotu had spent the next few days not directing warriors, but watching. Learning. Seeing how the demons fought, and how best to destroy them.

It had been difficult, particularly as they'd been fighting as a retreating line.

Finally, though, Chaotu and the others were moving forward.

This time would be different.

Chaotu knew he would never take Emil's place. Emil had been part of the LandHolder's family. A respected leader, whose brother was a brilliant tactician.

No, the best Chaotu could hope for was to become a leader of warriors himself, in his own right. To earn the trust of the VeinHolders.

While at the same time, not getting himself or too many of his warriors killed.

The call to push through the slowly moving curtain came. Ghosts swirled around the warriors, swelling the number of combatants.

Chaotu stepped forward.

The curtain itself always shocked him slightly. It was like crawling under a wool blanket in the middle of winter, when it would crackle and discharge sparks, making his hair stand on end.

At least he wore a heavy helmet, so he didn't have to push it back down. As well as light armor, magically enhanced, that would deflect most blows.

All of them had been warned that the land they were stepping onto had been changed by the ghosts. Though Kinaki had claimed it, his assertion was too new. It was easy enough for the ghosts to inhabit a large patch, to make it their own.

Chaotu marched with the rest of the army across the unsettled land. The warriors out front were from the House of Crystal, as they'd been working with unclaimed land more recently than any of the others. Then came the House of Pearl warriors, because they had not.

Chaotu hadn't been sure if his recent landless status would aid or hinder him. He was no longer tied to the House of Cobalt lands, but he hadn't acquired a sense of the House of Gold lands, either.

The screams of the warriors dying all around him drowned out his use of landsense. Instead, he focused on killing and on directing those around him to do the same. He probed the enemy's line and found soft spots, while at the same time worked to not fall into the traps that were much more obvious to him now.

He would not allow himself to get killed or even distracted.

Chaotu was one of the first to notice when the enemy forces began to withdraw. He kept his cheers to himself.

Instead, with grim determination, he pushed forward, driving them back further.

His arms ached with swinging his sword. His breath panted as the exhaustion that always seemed to bubble up came over him. The stench of gore churned his stomach.

Yet, underneath it all, instead of the constant smell of smoke and ash on the air, there appeared to be a fresh breeze blowing across the battlefield.

Chaotu finally felt his landsense start to awaken, in this unclaimed zone between Kinaki and Unnir. The land resented them both, was uninterested in the attachments of men. It would strive to remain free, if it could.

Would it always remain a haunted spot? Between the ghosts and the battle?

Chaotu would just have to survive the war to find out.

Chapter Eight
HOUSE OF PEARL

BENITOYO STILL WASN'T sure what had happened to him on the road traveling to Yawatan, the capital city of the lands of the House of Pearl. It had been such a strange dream. The man and the sliver of wood that he'd inserted into Benitoyo's palm, the way his blood had burned.

The feeling of a shadow covering his soul, making him both too warm and too cold at the same time.

Benitoyo had been feeling the weight of his deeds long before now. He'd been the one who'd poisoned Kinaki, making the LandHolder vulnerable to the demon. He'd distracted Sunli away from his proper duty, getting him to focus on useless details and never see the big picture. He'd also given Belam the false book, puffing up the priest, making him believe that he could call on demons from the underworld as well as control them.

But, as Ozukshi, Benitoyo's wife insisted, if he hadn't done it, someone else would have.

Instead, it had been him, and both he and his family had reaped the benefits of it. While Benitoyo and his wife stayed in their house in Yawatan, his three children had all made profitable marriages into good families, and were well on the way to becoming Holders, themselves.

That had been the primary reward that Benitoyo had pushed for, that the LandHolder grant his heirs their own land. He'd made his offspring work at their landsense ever since they were children, improving their natural abilities. Now, as adults, they should be strong enough to manage a small Hold, while their children would be stronger still.

And though Benitoyo didn't have much of a landsense (allowing him to work as a merchant in the House of Cobalt lands) it still felt good to be leaving the lands of the House of Cobalt, going back into the lands of the House of Pearl.

If only he felt better.

The darkness of his soul didn't appear to much care for the lands of the House of Pearl. The heaviness had increased after Benitoyo had crossed the border.

He assumed he'd just been tired. That, and the guards there had questioned him roughly, demanding to know his business, and why he'd stayed so long in the lands of the House of Cobalt.

He couldn't tell them he'd been working for Shimokoro, or committing crimes that the LandHolder had directed him to.

Though if Benitoyo was being completely honest, he'd never spoken with Darikuto. Not once. All his dealings were with Shimokoro. The priest had been very clever, issuing only verbal commands, never committing anything to writing.

But Benitoyo had been clever as well, documenting every meeting, as well as leaving notes for his heirs if something should happen to him unexpectedly.

Finally, though, all those deeds were behind him. Now, he could retire, spend time in the garden. There should be grandchildren soon to spoil.

When Benitoyo crested the last hill, he stepped to the

side of the road so he could look down on Yawatan for a few moments. The city was nestled at the bottom of the soft hills, with the gray ocean stretching out on the far side. It looked peaceful. The air was sweet, and the ground was solid underneath his feet. Blue sky domed overhead, with a sprinkling of white, fluffy clouds.

It felt good to be home.

A cloud crossed the sun before Benitoyo could take another step. Suddenly, the city was cast in shadow. Cold winds blew at Benitoyo, as if rebuffing him. The smell of ash —that awful smell that he'd become so accustomed to in the lands of the House of Cobalt—washed over him.

He shook his head. No, everything was fine here. He was just tired from his travels, as well as heartsore from his various deeds.

Everything was going to be just fine, now that he was home.

BENITOYO SAT in his well-appointed personal rooms. Glowing rocks in the hearth ate at the chill the early morning brought, but it wasn't enough. Benitoyo felt cold all the time. The chair he sat in had a tall back and had always been his favorite. Now, it was as if his body had changed, and it no longer fit him.

Nothing fit.

He still wasn't sure what sort of illness he'd come down with since he'd been back. First he was too hot, then too cold. A gray haze covered everything, stealing away the vibrant colors he so loved. He'd only managed to make love with Ozukshi the first night he'd been back, but hadn't touched her since.

What was wrong with him? It was as bad as the time he'd

tried the poison that he'd been feeding Kinaki, just to see what the effects truly were. He felt cut off from the land that should have welcomed him, cut off from his family and friends.

Even the gods seemed displeased. Like most merchants, Benitoyo had an altar to the God Xiuma in the corner. The statue had sat there for years, the god fat and happy, laughing from his throne. Benitoyo had always ensured that piles of gold coins and precious stones were strewn at the statue's feet.

But the second day after Benitoyo had returned, the head of the statue had just fallen off. No one had been near it at the time.

Horrified, Benitoyo had rushed out to the market to buy a new statue. A bigger, better one.

But then that hadn't fit on the pedestal that Benitoyo had been using, so he'd had to get a bigger table instead. He felt as though the altar was out of proportion with the rest of the room, taking up too much space.

The god's face wasn't the same either. Instead of laughing happily, he appeared to be sneering, though Ozukshi said Benitoyo was imagining it.

Benitoyo wasn't imagining the chill he constantly felt, except of course when he was wracked with fevers. They'd brought in the best healer they could find, but no one appeared to be able to fix whatever was wrong with Benitoyo. Normally, magic could take care of most illnesses.

Not this one.

Benitoyo knew that it was a sickness of his soul, all the deeds he'd done in service to The Plan coming back to haunt him.

He sat in his chair, uneasy. It was as if dinner the night before hadn't agreed with him. His felt bloated, and when he put his hand on his stomach, he could feel something sliding around inside of him, deeply unhappy.

Ozukshi had stayed in their shared bed that morning, feeling tired herself. Benitoyo feared that he'd given her whatever it was that he'd gotten. He was also worried about the marketplace. There appeared to be a mysterious illness spreading through there as well.

It had been one of the first places he'd gone when he'd returned, and then he'd gone back, several times.

They couldn't all be infected with his deeds, could they?

His stomach shifted around uncomfortably. For a moment, Benitoyo recalled when Ozukshi had been pregnant, and the sense of wonder he'd had touching her belly, feeling the new life moving inside of her.

The movements he felt now filled him with dread.

Nausea rose up swiftly. Benitoyo tried to rise from his chair but the world went black as he stood up and he fell to his knees, hard.

The jarring action was too much. Benitoyo spewed out the contents of his stomach onto the floor.

And more.

Horrified, Benitoyo saw those vines that he'd thought he'd left behind in the lands of the House of Cobalt writhing on the floor. Black beetles as long as his palm with sharp pincers scurried away from the mess. Corpse flowers rose up, blooming as soon as they reached the air, filling the room with an even worse stench.

But Benitoyo wasn't done. The infection had taken root deep inside of his body.

When he finished vomiting up the plants, insects, and filth that he'd carried with him from the House of Cobalt, he fell to the side, panting.

Gods, what had he done?

He could *see* how the plants would start to take over the

native species. How the deadly vines would choke off living things. Farmers' fields would be ruined. The famine would be widespread, though maybe it would be the lucky ones who would die.

Sharp, stabbing pain struck Benitoyo, in the belly. He groaned loudly and rolled over onto his back, sickened by how fast the plants were already growing.

He remembered the one insane temple attendant who he'd hired, who'd told him that the walls of the palace had been replaced with writhing, heaving vines.

He'd believed her.

Now, he was seeing the same thing occur in his own home, the plants shooting up and covering the walls, the books, the ceiling.

There would be no wood left once they took over.

The pain returned, making Benitoyo cry out. He put his hands on his seething belly, feeling it pulse with an alien beat. The pain brought tears to his eyes, though he recalled his wife's admonishment that men knew nothing of pain of childbirth.

He tried to laugh. To catch his breath. To tell his wife one last time that he loved her.

The searing agony stole away last words.

He thought he felt the sides of his belly tear, like an overripe fruit, spewing forth its seeds.

The bad seeds.

He knew his body would provide fertile ground for the deadly tree sure to take root, that he had given birth to.

A haunted tree, that demons would use to climb out of the underworld.

Benitoyo had thought that he'd left all his bad deeds behind, that what he'd done to further The Plan wouldn't affect him, or the House of Pearl. Not in a bad way.

But he'd carried the seeds of destruction unknowingly with him.

How many others had been infected, the same as he had been?

How soon before Yawatan became the same stinking, awful place that Jinyi had become?

Benitoyo didn't know. He wouldn't be alive to see the consequences of his deeds.

He died in pain, all alone, knowing that he'd failed not his LandHolder, but the entire world.

Chapter Nine
HOUSE OF CRYSTAL

MENHAPTU GRUMBLED with the rest about the forced march all the way across the lands of the House of Gold. Yimifut had initially brought the entire force with him in a single step, to get to the border.

It had taken an unbelievable amount of strength, as well as magic, to do that. Menhaptu had been impressed despite himself.

Yimifut appeared to be a young man, only in his teens still. But he had more power than anyone Menhaptu had ever met.

The trip across the House of Gold lands had been unsettling. Menhaptu tried to keep at least some of his complaints to himself. He couldn't help it, though! It just was all so unheard of, this great attack of one house against another.

And what would happen to the House of Crystal? The LandHolder shouldn't be leaving so soon. It would weaken his hold on the land.

It seemed also that Menhaptu had misjudged the

importance of that girl, Akalina. She and her sister appeared to be well-acquainted with the new LandHolder.

He had little satisfaction over the realization that she had, indeed, brought some of the ghosts from the House of Crystal with her. He'd been right about her, in that regard.

Yet, that left the House of Crystal weaker as well.

If only Menhaptu had had the chance to explain to Yimifut how dangerous his actions were! What a mistake he was making!

These children were just too impetuous.

Menhaptu stood with the other heads of temples off to one side as the warriors prepared that morning to cross the curtain that marked the border.

He wondered idly what sort of curtain Yimifut might raise to separate off the House of Crystal from the other lands.

The image came to him quickly—a border defended by ghosts and winds from the mountain. A solid white wall that chilled whoever passed through it to their very soul.

He shivered, glad that they hadn't come to that.

At least, not yet.

Torja, the head of the Temple of Truth for the House of Gold stood to the side. He'd tried to give her a wide berth as well. Instead of the stately being he'd expected, in the traditional fine, long robes of the House of Gold, she wore a loose fitting dress made out of a flimsy pale green cloth that seemed to billow on winds he couldn't feel. While her tiny breasts were covered with patches of cloth, the rest of her chest was bare, along with her shoulders and arms.

She was younger as well. She'd sought different paths of divination, much more aggressively than Menhaptu ever had.

And had more luck as well.

After the priests and priestesses had blessed the various

contingents of warriors, they stayed where they were while the warriors pressed through the curtain.

The screams that arose sent shivers down Menhaptu's spine.

He'd never heard good people die like that before.

"It's the demons," Torja said, sliding up to stand beside him.

It would have helped if she'd been short, so that she had at least a possibility of being demure. However, she was taller than he was, almost a full head's worth. He found himself staring at her bare throat, and if he wasn't careful, her barely restrained breasts.

"Hmmm?" Menhaptu said, forcing his eyes up to hers.

She seemed to be amused by him, despite the sounds of fierce battle just beyond the golden shimmering veil.

"The demons don't just tear apart a warrior's body, but also their soul," she said calmly, as if it were common knowledge and the most ordinary thing in the world. "So many of the warriors are getting destroyed completely."

"Good heavens! Are you sure?" Menhaptu said, the implications striking home.

If the warriors' souls were being destroyed, it meant they couldn't go into the underworld. They would never find the River Guanaliki, then follow its course to the grand ocean of light and be carried away to the Golden Lands.

It also meant that none of them would return as ghosts either, their souls afraid to enter the underworld.

Fewer ghosts meant less magic, as well as fewer foretellings.

Torja nodded. "Yes. Too many souls are being destroyed. We will all feel the loss."

Her eyes darted to the side, to where Darikuto stood with the others. He had a look of complete concentration on his face as he directed his PearlHolders, listened to messengers about the state of the battle, and made suggestions.

All the LandHolders supported their warriors as best they could, though the lands they fought on were foreign.

And some of the land was unclaimed, now, thanks to the ghosts.

"How did it get to this point?" Menhaptu said. He thought back to the Chamber of Crystals, and how it had been corrupted.

"Darikuto has been directing us toward this confrontation for years, now," Torja said darkly. "I saw it."

Menhaptu swallowed his instant denial. If the head of the Temple of Truth saw something, it would be true.

But why would one of the LandHolders actively work against the others?

Even as he posed the question to himself, he knew the answer.

Land.

Every LandHolder always wanted more.

"Did he believe he could become the sole LandHolder?" Menhaptu asked quietly.

"I think so," Torja said.

"What will we do with him, once we beat Kinaki?" Menhaptu said.

"No one knows," Torja replied grimly. "And none can see the path clearly."

Menhaptu sighed, feeling the truth of that too well.

Menhaptu didn't bother eating after midday. While there had been a mood of celebration served with the noonday meal, it had been short-lived.

The border was being slowly pushed out again, back

toward its original location. What they'd lost in a single day was going to take weeks, perhaps months, to regain, though. Even the help of the ghosts hadn't been enough.

Then the wounded had started to return. Men and women fevered and delirious. They didn't just have physical injuries, but some sort of sickness of the soul.

Menhaptu's greatest strength had never been healing others. No, he was good at reading the smoke from incense, as well as hearing the voices and words cast by the crystals.

He'd always thought of his ability as his only power, that he'd been the ones shifting the veils between past, present, and future.

Now, he had a much better understanding that it wasn't just him. No, he'd been working with the ghosts to see.

He watched, fascinated, as Torja whirled, drawing up the smoke from incense normally burned for the ghosts and flinging it around. Not many could see the ghosts that would be attracted to her, or hear the words whispered in her ear.

Was this to become the new form of foretelling? This sort of dance? While Torja had a level of grace, he knew that he'd look like a great fool trying such a thing.

Then again, those elders at the temple, who'd thrust Menhaptu forward so that he could fail and they'd be blame-free, wouldn't take to this new form well either.

Pain appeared to fill Torja's eyes as her dance faltered and she slowed.

Pain that spilled out to the surrounding hillside. Everyone grew still.

"The disease spreads," she announced. "And we are going to have to cut out the rot."

Menhaptu shivered, afraid of what that entailed, and how deep the cuts were going to have to go.

Chapter Ten
HOUSE OF COBALT

꧁꧂

KINAKI TRIED to share the feeling of the *Land* with Wanho, but the demon didn't appear to appreciate it, not like Kinaki did.

Every time Unnir pulled back her border, leaving *unclaimed land* behind, Kinaki had wallowed in the feeling of new land, new territory, being added to the House of Cobalt lands. He felt drunk with it, giddy in a way he hadn't felt for quite some time.

Wanho pushed them forward when Kinaki would have taken his time. Given a chance, he would have moved forward a single step, then stopped, relishing the expansion he felt as his landsense delved into the ground and he marked every rock with his name. Only after a time would he have taken the next step.

But they were chasing an army. They had battles to fight. Kinaki could spend time with his new territory later.

Except—there wasn't to be a later.

That damned Unnir had laid the perfect trap for him, using ghosts to free some of the land that Kinaki had claimed. Of course it had taken all his attention, drawing it away from the warriors when they needed it most.

And those damned ghosts. Where had they come from?

Wanho had explained that ghosts were the natural enemy of the demons. When a priest or priestess did a foretelling, the ghosts not only aided them, they also protected them.

It was why so few ghosts had remained in the lands of the House of Cobalt. The demons hadn't slaughtered all of them, but as many as they could find. The rest of the ghosts had gone into hiding.

Ghosts fight for the living, Wanho had explained. *Demons fight for the dead.*

Kinaki had successfully hidden his unease at that.

Did Wanho consider Kinaki to be dead? Was that why the demons fought for him?

Or did they only fight for their own kind? For Wanho? Did they no longer fight for Kinaki at all?

Pulling back, losing the land that he'd so newly acquired, had left Kinaki feeling maddened. He howled back behind the lines that night, feeling cramped and bound.

It had been so nice to have that itch for new territory finally scratched!

He growled as he paced at the head of the large banquet tent, set up every night for all the warriors to gather, eat and drink together, sharing their great victories. The only table was at the front, for Kinaki to sit at. The rest of the warriors stood in groups as they ate and drank, served by nimble servants weaving between them.

Would you sit already?

Kinaki nearly smiled at how, well, like the living that the demon now sounded.

It was also telling that Wanho didn't just take over their body and make Kinaki follow Wanho's wishes.

While Kinaki had given up some things after the end of their great battle in the underworld, he still felt as though Wanho had given up more.

Kinaki sat. Sour wine was fetched for him immediately. He grabbed a handful of slugs and ate those as well, relishing how they still wiggled in his mouth, how they slid around and down his throat.

Then he noticed that there appeared to be fewer warriors gathered together that night. Had they lost that many? He thought back to the battles. No, the losses were about the same as they'd always been.

Still, he had to ask one of the minions who was racing from group to group, serving wine and raw meat.

The servant seemed dumbstruck that the LandHolder, himself, was addressing him.

"Sire! I mean, Holder! I mean, LandHolder! Yes! There are fewer warriors here tonight. Some were struck by a fever, earlier. But they'll be better soon! Yes!"

With that, the servant hurried away.

"Fever?" Kinaki said. Though he spoke the question out loud, he directed his query inward.

You'll see came the smug reply.

That unsettled Kinaki more than he cared to admit. "What exactly will I see?" he asked.

You're so attracted to the land, Wanho replied. *I wanted to make it extra special for you.*

Kinaki drank a bit more wine, sending his landsense down and all around him. They were still in the territory that he'd only recently claimed. The land was strong, and held a lot of magic. It was heady to draw power from it, like sipping the first ice wine of the season, sweet and chilled.

To the side, he felt something else start to take root. Something that wasn't him, or his will. He stood in alarm.

Relax, Wanho said, forcing their body back down. *You've gone and ruined the surprise.*

Kinaki kept his attention on the area. He finally realized what Wanho was doing.

The gorgeous plants and vines that now took up much of the lands of the House of Cobalt had been sadly missing here, in the House of Gold.

Seemed Wanho had found a way to bring those here, to have them breach the surface.

The feeling of losing the land increased. Kinaki suddenly recognized the corruption taking place.

Wanho wasn't weakening Kinaki by bringing those plants here, to this newly acquired territory.

The demon was, however, increasing his own strength.

The corruption of the House of Cobalt had been gradual, and Kinaki's misgivings had been undermined by the delight of the demon in all the beautifully colored flowers that were growing everywhere.

Now, Kinaki could feel the difference.

It wasn't good.

He tried to hide his feelings from Wanho, however. "That is quite a surprise!" he said. "How did you manage to bring the vines and the plants here?"

It is much easier to corrupt the flesh of the living than the land itself, Wanho admitted.

Kinaki saw the procedure that Wanho had developed. How he'd managed to take a sliver of a demon's soul, manifest it in the land of the living, then insert it into one of the living themselves. The demon wouldn't be reborn, no, but as the body died, it would become a bridge to the underworld.

"I see," Kinaki said. "Soon, we will take over all the lands. Turn them into a paradise, like the House of Cobalt."

Exactly! Wanho seemed especially pleased with himself.

Kinaki signaled for another bottle of wine to be brought to him as he pondered whether or not he had gone too far in his reach for land.

And if it was too late.

Chapter Eleven
HOUSE OF GOLD

TORJA WOULD HAVE WEPT, but she felt wrung out of tears.

What she'd seen had baked her soul into a hard nugget, no longer pure gold but now with added steel.

No one could have foretold what being the head priestess of the Temple of Truth during this time would do to her.

And despite how she missed the more innocent, youthful side of herself, she knew that the gods were tempering her to become what she needed to be.

No matter how painful the consequences might be to her, personally.

It was partly why she wore such a fanciful, light outfit now, when she did her foretelling dance. Her old robes were too heavy and restricting. Besides, dressing in provocative gauze was a surefire way to get people to underestimate her. Not as if they'd ever stopped doing that.

At least Unnir would listen to her.

"We need to isolate the warriors who are fevered," Torja announced to all of those gathered on the hillside to hear the latest foretelling. "Keep them separate from the others. No healers shall enter their tent. No priests or priestesses either."

"What, we should just push them off to the side? Leave them to die?" someone challenged her.

Torja thought it might be the GuildHolder for the healers. She sighed, then nodded. "Some of them will die. Yes. But better that they die alone, than that they infect the others."

The vision she'd seen had been of bodies, corpulent and rotting, providing fertile ground for those horrible plants of the underworld. Only the cleansing fire would uproot those. They'd have to purify the ground where the tent was erected, once those who had passed had gone to seed. She'd salt the earth as well. Maybe put a ring of salt around the tent once they'd sealed it off.

Salt was how you got rid of slugs, right? And she'd never forgotten that image of the Holder Slug, who'd taken off with her fletche in the first place.

Torja turned toward the LandHolders, who were still directing the battle on the far side of the curtain.

Should she tell Darikuto? About the bad seeds that had already taken root in the lands of the House of Pearl?

She didn't want to. Let him go and stew in his own rot. He'd been the cause of this mess to start with.

However, too many innocents would die if she said nothing. And her heart hadn't hardened that much, it seemed.

"Darikuto!" Torja called out, drawing the LandHolder's attention to herself.

She still wanted to spit every time she looked at the man. But they needed him. Unnir needed his warriors if they were to ever beat Kinaki.

"People in your land have already been infected," she said. "In Yawatan. You will need to send a messenger to burn out the area."

He glared at her. Probably didn't approve of her outfit, or

of a mere priestess telling the Great Grand LandHolder what to do.

Too bad.

Torja could tell that the GuildHolder of the healers wanted to argue with Torja about her vision. Ragna rescued her, though.

"Here, drink this," Ragna said, roughly shoving a wine bottle into Torja's hands.

Fortunately, the bottle was filled with water, with both a touch of honey as well as salt in it. Torja found herself guzzling the entire thing down, the cool water sending chills through her body.

"Thank you," Torja said, handing the bottle back to Ragna.

Before the GuildHolder could get a word in edgewise, Ragna took hold of Torja's arm and said, "You must be exhausted. Come. You need to rest."

"But the foretelling!" the GuildHolder cried out.

Ragna pulled herself up to her full height and looked down her nose at the GuildHolder. "You've heard what the head priestess had to say. The infection must be cut out. Separate the warriors as you've been instructed. Or pay the consequence as the disease spreads and all of us die."

The GuildHolder gulped and stepped back, nodding but still looking stubborn.

Stupid man. He'd get them all killed with his kind heart.

"She's right," Torja said. "I know, it's hard. It's a pain we must all bear. But we have to separate out those who are fevered. Right now."

A warrior suddenly appeared at Torja's side. She winked at the priestess, then turned a somber mien to the GuildHolder. "I will help you," she said. Her tone brooked no opposition.

The GuildHolder just sighed and shuffled off, still arguing but at least starting to move.

Ragna took a moment to look at Torja. "You're still too pale," she announced. "You need to rest."

Before Torja could say anything more, Ragna held up her hand. "You can talk and tell us all about your vision. I'll have a scribe there to record all your words. But you don't have to do it here, standing on the hillside with all the others. You need to sit. And rest."

Torja sighed. The exhaustion hadn't hit her yet—she was still running on the thrill of the foretelling, on the natural high she got from the dance.

Soon, though, her tiredness would land on her head like a sack of ore. She needed to speak of all she'd seen before that happened.

With a tired nod, she let herself be led away. It was better she rest now, as she was certain her nightmares would keep her up for quite a while later that evening.

Chapter Twelve
HOUSE OF PEARL

CHUYOKO WAS DISGUSTED at the order to isolate the fevered warriors. These were *her* people. Her warriors. Her PearlHolders of all their various ranks and positions.

It made no damned sense. Surely they had priests or healers who could reduce the fevers, make those who were sick well again.

Chuyoko paced back and forth outside the damned tent, occasionally talking to those inside who were in her charge. She listened to the moans of those who were sickest. She wanted to charge the tent. It wouldn't withstand a single blow of her sword. Rescue those who were inside.

She didn't. She also knew how to follow an order, and this one came from the LandHolder himself.

This wasn't the time to challenge him, or to talk of their broken trust. Not yet. She'd seen how he'd fought that day with the others. He was still a good leader. She wasn't certain that she trusted him, though, and standing on that precipitous hill made her uneasy.

Though she'd been fighting all day, with everyone else, she would not rest. She would not permit herself to feel her exhaustion. She had compromised, and gone down to her lightest leathers. She didn't have a bow and arrow, though she knew how to use one. Instead, she had a supply of javelins that she'd stuck into the ground, in a line, as if daring anyone to come closer.

She paced a good ten feet away from the tent containing the worst of those who were sick. She would see that they stayed inside, as well as make sure that none visited.

At least the first night.

Come the second night, she might have a very different mission, namely, rescuing those who were inside.

An unearthly howl split the night.

Chuyoko had to fight against her instinct to rush toward the tent, to run into danger. Instead, she hurried over to her javelins, pulling one out of the ground.

A figure tugged aside one of the tent flaps. He glared outside, then down at his feet.

Chuyoko had thought it odd that they used up all the salt in the entire camp to draw a circle around the tent itself. Torja had mentioned something about containing slugs, which had made no sense at all.

However, the warrior before her seemed unable to cross it.

Chuyoko didn't know the person. He was from one of the other Houses. He swayed where he was standing, both hands wrapped around his belly as if trying to assuage the pain brought on by an overly rich meal.

He shuddered, then spewed vomit. Much of it landed outside the circle of the tent.

Immediately, those awful vines that Chuyoko had seen in the lands of the House of Cobalt sprang up.

She pulled out a short dagger, carrying it as well as the javelin, and rushed forward, ready to cut them to pieces.

Another of the guards beat her there, pouring salt over the plants instead.

They wilted under the onslaught.

Chuyoko returned her attention to the figure in the door. He'd fallen back. Even in the dim light, Chuyoko could see the way that *things* crawled under his skin.

Without hesitation, Chuyoko threw her javelin, catching the figure in the throat.

It was too late. His belly still burst from the ill seed he carried.

More vines. More deadly plants. The whiff of ashes and corruption wafted from the tent.

Chuyoko looked at the other guard, a warrior from the House of Gold.

They had the same look of grim determination in their eyes.

Another piercing shriek came from inside the tent.

More foulness being spewed onto the ground.

Was it better to kill them all? Would any of those who were fevered survive?

Chuyoko understood that the priestess could not have ordered the warriors to slaughter their own. Not before they saw the evidence of what their fellow comrades carried.

With a nod, the other guard called to some of her followers.

Grimly, they entered the tent, the foul stench of those who'd already succumbed filling the enclosed space, making Chuyoko's eyes water.

One by one, Chuyoko and the guards killed all of those who were too far gone, giving them a kinder death than exploding from the inside of the foulness they carried.

They agreed to wait for the others, the ones who still had only a slight fever, to see if they would survive the night.

In the end, they killed all but one of the three dozen warriors in the tent.

CHUYOKO TRIED TO REST, at least for a few hours, before the next day of fighting began. Her body needed sleep. She lay in her plain tent, on a plain cot, eyes closed but sleep a good distance away.

As far as they could tell, none of the guards who'd worked with Chuyoko that night had been infected by the Fevered, as they'd started to call them. They weren't sure how it was transferred, but all of the Fevered had had major cuts. Perhaps once the skin was broken, the fever could take hold.

It had been an awful thing to behold. Terrible acts that Chuyoko had had to perform. To kill her own warriors, as each of the guards insisted on taking care of their own, rather than leave their fate with a stranger.

At least none of those injured begged to live. Instead, they'd begged for death, before they were too far gone.

Chuyoko turned over onto her side, going through her warrior stretches in her mind, seeking some sort of release for herself.

Because otherwise her thoughts kept circling back to Darikuto. Her LandHolder. The one she'd dedicated most of her life to.

The one who was responsible for where they were that day. Who could be held accountable for all of those brave warriors' lives she'd had to take.

Chuyoko understood battles and war. She knew that lives would be lost if The Plan was going to bear fruit.

She'd just not anticipated this sort of rotten fruit.

Perhaps she should have, knowing that Darikuto was going to be flirting with demons.

That was the other thing that bothered her. The priestess had also foreseen that similar things were happening in Yawatan. Others who bore the same fever, who were probably dying with the same disastrous results.

As far as Chuyoko knew, Darikuto hadn't sent any messengers back to the city, warning them to of the encroaching disease.

She was just going to have to send one of her own warriors back with strict orders how to deal with the infestation.

The House of Pearl, with its long coast, had warehouses full of salt. Those would have to be accessed first, handed out to all the guard.

Decision made, Chuyoko felt herself finally drifting off.

The fact that she was going behind the back of the LandHolder seemed to not bother her in the least.

Because she knew, deep in her heart, that it was the Land she was protecting. And that was all that mattered.

Chapter Thirteen
HOUSE OF CRYSTAL

Yimifut sat in his tent that evening, listening in the distance to the terrible cries of the warriors as they died from the fever. He'd taken some time to study the warriors who'd been afflicted. Some, though not all, of their auras held an ashy layer to them, a pale sickly white that didn't seem natural.

He knew he needed to sleep, but that might be a while in coming. He drank some watered wine, hoping that would help in a bit.

No matter how he sat, he was still uncomfortable. Not because of the chair, no.

His hold on the land was fading.

That first night, it had been like slipping into the most comfortable wool robe, sitting in the perfect chair, and sipping warmed mead in front of a huge fire. The Land surrounded him, supported him, comforted him, loved him, in its own fashion.

Though parts of the land that had broken free had grown wild and resentful of the living, they'd been more like petulant children being brought to bed after a long day of playing, rather than willful rebels who'd had enough of everything.

Now, though, Yimifut could feel the robe sliding off, or perhaps growing thin and threadbare. The fire wasn't as warm, either, and his toes were getting cold. The sweet mead had grown sour, like poorly aged wine that had turned to vinegar. And he no longer sat comfortably either, but on a hard, rocky surface.

Yimifut suspected that it would get worse before it got better.

If he would ever feel completely comfortable with his own land again.

He could hate Darikuto for making him agree to come and give Unnir aid. Then again, he had planned on coming to help anyway.

Plus, he was operating blindly. He'd always had a good idea of what was going to happen, if not the details, at least the broad outline.

Things were too close to call. He didn't know if he would survive the war, or if someone else might be called to be LandHolder in his stead.

But he would do what needed doing, no matter the cost, to ensure that the land survived. That had been his promise as he'd taken on the mantle.

Yimifut shifted again on his chair, sighing, wishing the foresight he'd had in his youth had remained.

Then he snorted at himself. He was still a youth, still untried. He'd only taken on the mantle of the land for a few days, now. But he felt much, much older now.

He heard a soft knock on the wooden post standing beside the tent flap, put there for that purpose, so someone could knock before entering.

"Come in," he said.

His heart was soothed when he saw Befery had pulled

back the tent flap. She carried a tray that held a teapot and cups.

Without asking, she bustled into the tent, placing the tray down on the table.

"I figured you'd be having some difficulty sleeping," Befery said. "Just like I was. So I made us some tea."

Yimifut smiled at her and pushed his wine glass to the side. "Aye," he said. "Thank you."

He knew that most LandHolders had servants who took care of them. Holder Sitre had some servants who took care of the Hold, but she did most of the work herself, along with others.

Not that he considered Befery a servant. No, she was like a big sister taking care of her slightly stupid younger brother, who didn't have the sense to come in out of the rain.

He wrapped his hands around the cup of tea she poured him, inhaling the sweet scent of peppermint mingled with the earthy smell of chamomile. "Thank you," he said again. "I don't know what I'd do without you here."

"Do?" Befery snorted. "You'd work yourself to the bone, probably collapsing on the battlefield come midday. You need someone practical in your life, to take care of you."

Yimifut nodded. She was probably right.

"If we survive this, will you come and work for me?" Yimifut felt himself asking.

"No," Befery said, making Yimifut feel even more stupid. "I have my own family to raise. But we'll see each other. I'll make you tea sometimes."

"Will you help me find the right people?" he said seriously.

"You can read auras," Befery pointed out. "You don't really need me. Or anyone else." She reached across the table and squeezed his hand briefly before letting go. "It's lonely being a LandHolder. Or so it seems like from here. The land can only comfort you so much."

Yimifut nodded, afraid to say what was on his mind, how the land wouldn't be there for him.

"Now, I know you're afraid of losing the land," Befery said.

It shouldn't surprise him that she knew what he was thinking, but it did. He took too big of a gulp of tea, scorching his mouth. He soothed the hurt an instant later, but he knew she'd seen it.

"You're going to be all right," Befery assured him. "The land will still be there when you get back. You may have to fight harder for it. Go on Promenade or something. But you'll still be the LandHolder. Just the land may be different."

"Go on," Yimifut said. She'd seen through the gist of it—he'd been afraid of his hold on the land, not of how the land itself would be changing.

Befery sighed. "I don't have a tremendous amount of magic. Or a great landsense. Akalina was always much stronger than me or our other sister."

Yimifut nodded, encouraging Befery to gather her thoughts.

"There's some connection between the ghosts and the magic, right? And foretelling?"

"Yes," Yimifut said. "Though no one has really paid much heed to it, as there's always been more than enough magic in the land. As well as more than enough ghosts."

"The other houses don't have a ghost court," Befery said. "They don't have as much understanding of their past as we do."

"Why does that matter?" Yimifut said, confused at this point by how the conversation had veered.

"We know what the past was like. So we don't step

forward easily into the future," Befery said after a few moments. "You're afraid you're losing the land, that it's slipping away from you. And it might be. We've all heard the stories and myths about wandering LandHolders who lose control of their land."

Before Yimifut could say anything, Befery continued. "But. Right now, you want to go back to the land. To hold it. To be held by it. True?"

"Yes," Yimifut breathed out. "Oh, so true." He ached with the loss, with it being so far away.

"Good," Befery said firmly. "Then you'll get it back, no problem. However, the land is going to be changed. According to Akalina, there might not be as much magic there."

"That's true," Yimifut said.

"And how is that going to affect the LandHolder?" Befery said seriously.

Yimifut blinked, taken aback. "I don't know," he said after a few moments.

"That's right. You don't know. No one knows. And worrying about it isn't going to change that fact. You'll get the land back. Then you'll have to discover what exactly that means."

"I see," Yimifut said. "You're right. The shape of the land will have changed. Just as the shape of the lands for the other houses."

"Even the House of Pearl?" Befery asked bluntly. "Because it seems to me that they have caused the most damage, and have lost the least."

Yimifut swallowed hard. He agreed with Befery, that Darikuto's plan had brought them all to this place of ruin.

But they needed him, and his warriors. Plus, it was just Yimifut and Unnir, both relatively new LandHolders. They couldn't oust Darikuto, not yet.

"We have to focus on the enemy at hand, first," Yimifut said after a few moments. "Then we'll turn our attention to the House of Pearl and Darikuto. You have my word."

"Thank you, LandHolder," Befery said formally. She smiled at him, drinking down the last of her tea. "And now I can sleep, because you will do the right thing. I know that."

Yimifut smiled at her, then surprisingly enough, found himself yawning.

"Go to bed," Befery told him sternly as she cleaned up the teapot and cups. "Tomorrow will come soon enough."

Sleepily, Yimifut nodded, taking himself to the back of the tent and throwing himself down on his cot.

Just before sleep grabbed hold of him, Yimifut marveled again at the woman he'd never foreseen, whose council was the one he needed most. He had no romantic intentions toward her—she was already married, with children of her own. And none of her children were old enough to marry either, to keep their family lines close.

Still, there had to be something he could give her in way of gratitude, later, after they'd won the war.

After he'd learned the new shape of his land.

Chapter Fourteen
HOUSE OF COBALT

FAKRA LIFTED the heavy iron digging pole far above her head and slammed it back down into the heart of the corrupt vine trying to take root in her hold.

She missed, of course.

Damned thing was slippery. She knew that it was only in her dreams that she could see the plants actually moving, stalking around her hold, searching for a weak spot to attack. Or the really awful nightmares where they isolated all of her land and then came in for the kill.

Fakra wiggled the bar back and forth, at least loosening the roots of the stupid plant. It was hot work, even in the late summer afternoon shade. She paused for a moment, using the sleeve of her plain gray shirt to wipe at the sweat gathered across her forehead. Her pants were short and ended just below her knee, and they were pasted to her thighs with sweat. At least her once black hair—now mostly silver—was now long enough to wear in a single braid down her back.

Fighting off the corrupt plants was a continual battle. Fortunately, she was used to that. Fakra had fought long and hard as a warrior for Kinaki, back when he'd been a proper

75

LandHolder. She didn't trust the changes she'd seen, and had gotten out early, though she'd been a respected CollierHolder with many years ahead of her.

She bent her knees slightly, then straightened them, holding on to the digging bar and wrenching it from the earth. The digging bar was made out of solid metal and over six feet long, a good half a foot taller than she was. She used it instead of a javelin sometimes to practice her warrior exercises.

Mostly, though, she just used it for digging out the corrupt plants that crept into her Hold.

She'd been in her late forties when she'd retired to the small Hold the LandHolder had granted her. It had surprised her as much as anyone that she had such a good landsense, good enough to be able to hold onto this much land.

Then again, she understood that all movement came from the feet. She always planted herself firmly when she was doing her warrior exercises in the morning, grounding herself. That way, she wouldn't be easily knocked over, despite her smaller stature.

She drew the digging bar up over her head again, then paused, feeling for the *wrongness* of the plant using her landsense. She couldn't trust her eyes sometimes. The damned things *did* appear to slide away from her.

Ah. There.

Fakra struck the head of the digging bar into the heart of the vine, spearing it mightily. She felt it wither around the edges of the steel.

Good.

It didn't take long, now, to uproot the damned thing, digging up all its tendrils and vines. She had a cloth tucked into the waist of her pants, which she now wrapped around her hand before reaching for the vine, tugging the ugly thing out of the ground.

She threw it onto the pile that had steadily grown all afternoon. Once she was finished, she'd set the pile on fire, then the next morning, scatter the ashes around the border of her Hold. That appeared to keep the vines back, tasting the ashes of their companions.

At least for a short while.

Every day, she'd had to spend time clearing the edges of her Hold from the incursion of the corrupt plants.

She no longer tried to bring her cattle to the market in Jinyi. People weren't buying fresh meat. She'd slaughtered many of her cows and salted the meat away. She'd also stocked up her Hold with plenty of flour and other goods that she could conjure herself, but were easier to have on hand.

Just fifteen families worked with her in her Hold. They'd diversified their crops years before, so that they could be a mostly self-sufficient Hold.

Fakra tried to protect them from whatever weird corrupt plants tried to creep in. Others in the Hold now worked the portion of the land that she'd formerly farmed, just so that she could spend her time in battle.

The corruption wasn't just at her Hold, though. It was taking place across the breadth of the lands of the House of Cobalt.

If Fakra thought it would do any good, she'd go complain to Kinaki about it.

However, as she suspected that the land was merely reflecting the current state of the LandHolder, there wasn't anything she could do.

Except to do battle every day, and hope that at some point, the land itself would get sick of how it was being used and would flee the current LandHolder.

Fakra didn't envy the next LandHolder, not in the least.

It would be a near-impossible task to clean up what had once been a fertile, pleasant land.

All she could do for now was to keep her own small portion of it clean.

The last plant finally dug up for the day, Fakra set the piles of vines on fire, sending the flames high as a signal not just to the family whose lands she'd worked that day that their borders were now clean, but to any who were thinking about coming this way.

Fakra would be ready for them, ready to do battle again. Tomorrow, and every day.

Chapter Fifteen
HOUSE OF GOLD

❧

VIDE TRIED his best to function, despite Emil's death. It felt as though he was trying to run with a broken ankle, or keeping his wits despite drinking a half dozen bottles of wine.

He felt as though he worked in bits and starts. For the briefest of moments, he would be able to think. He'd shine with brilliance, enlightening all of those around him.

The rest of the time, it was just a slough to get through every day. He'd find himself stopping, saying to himself, *I must remember to share that with Emil later on.* Or he'd be drinking a particularly good vintage of wine, and would want to go give Emil a taste.

Or even, as was more usual, when someone said or did something particularly stupid, and Vide still had no Emil to tell.

It was worse than any nightmare.

Unnir had chided him, shamed him to his feet. So at least he was mobile, now, instead of crawling into a bottle and staying there.

But she couldn't bring any joy to the world. Not even

when they'd finally started pushing Kinaki and his thrice-damned warriors back. The border for the House of Gold merely inched forward.

It was going to take months of long, nasty fighting. So many more people would die. Other people's brothers, or cousins, or wives, or daughters.

He had to figure out how to end this battle, once and for all. He was brilliant, after all. Surely he could come up with a plan?

He knew now that much of his former brilliance hadn't come from himself, but rather, had been a light shining off Emil's solid presence.

He wasn't completely lost without his brother.

However, at the same time, Vide hadn't found himself either.

It was why he'd asked to speak with Lijun, one of Kinaki's children and former heirs. He couldn't bring himself to speak to Chaotu. He knew himself well enough to realize that he'd just end up yelling at the stupid idiot who'd gotten Emil killed.

Talking to his sister was going to be bad enough.

Vide had gone back to his fastidious ways. The rug that covered the floor of his tent was immaculate, the fibers even fluffy, though Vide would never admit to sometimes walking barefoot across it, just to feel the softness of it. All the wine bottles had been removed and the air freshened. Notes and maps were neatly stacked to one side of his table. He had a tea service sitting there instead, with a crisp green tea that cleared the senses, while at the same time, kept him grounded.

He wore one of the more casual robes that the people from the House of Gold had appeared to have adopted due to circumstances. Instead of a greenish-gray robe with sleeves cuffs that, when held at the waist, reached all the way to his knees, he wore a simple green tabard over a tightly fitted white shirt, belted together with solid leather. Like some of the others, he now wore a badge about the side of his palm stitched to the center of his chest, made out of an intricate pattern of green and gold braided ribbons. His trousers were plain black, with good solid boots.

The guard at Vide's tent stuck his head in, making sure that Vide was presentable (at least in appearance) before announcing that Lijun had arrived and holding the tent flap back for her to enter.

Vide had originally grilled both Lijun and Chaotu for whatever actionable information they could give him about Kinaki and his armies. However, while Lijun hadn't been in hiding, Chaotu had been. He'd even faked his own death so that his father would stop sending assassins after him.

They'd crossed the House of Cobalt lands led by some sort of weird amalgamation of demon and the living, the head of the Temple of Truth. Lijun had been truly upset at his death.

But one more person from the House of Cobalt being dead made no difference to Vide.

Lijun's cheeks looked ruddy, like most of those from the House of Cobalt. She was at least a head shorter than Vide, and her bones seemed slight. She wore her black hair pulled back severely from her face, tied up tightly in a long braid that went down to the center of her back.

That she wore a more formal robe in the style of the House of Gold surprised Vide. Then again, she'd given up her claim on the lands of the House of Cobalt, as Chaotu had. Her dark brown eyes held as much sorrow as Vide's cool gray ones. And her smile seemed pasted on, as if she didn't want to be meeting him any more than he wanted to speak with her.

Still, Vide was politeness itself. "Welcome," he said,

standing up and then escorting her to the table. "I have tea for us," he added, picking up the finely made clay teapot and swirling the contents once.

"Thank you," Lijun said. She held out her cup for him to pour.

"You're welcome," Vide said, pouring them both a cup, then not sure where to begin.

Emil had always been much better with people than Vide had been. He knew how to talk with anyone.

Vide was better at sneering at everyone.

"I suppose you wonder why I asked you here today," Vide said.

"No, not at all," Lijun said. She looked at him directly. "You want to know if there's a way to trap the LandHolder. Some scheme that you can use to end the war more quickly."

Vide blinked, surprised. Lijun had always struck him as being passive, standing to the side and letting others do what needed doing.

"That is correct," he said. "Do you have any ideas?"

"I do, actually," Lijun said. Her keen gaze pinned him in place. "Why should I tell you?"

"I beg your pardon?" Vide said, even more surprised. "Why shouldn't you tell me?"

"You hate me," Lijun said. She didn't say it angrily, but more matter of fact. "You despise Chaotu. You blame him for the death of your brother."

Vide didn't see any point in denying what she was saying. "I do blame Chaotu," he said directly. "Your brother was being an idiot, and then my idiot brother had to go and rescue him."

"My brother can be an idiot sometimes, yes," Lijun said simply. "But he has the right heart. I'm afraid, though, that the plan I've come up with will put him into danger. More danger. And that you will see to it that he is killed in the ensuing battle, somehow."

Vide took a deep breath and nodded. He contemplated his tea for a moment before he took a large sip. It had cooled slightly, and was turning bitter.

"I'm not going to deny that would be a rather nice enticement to me," he said plainly. "To kill both Kinaki and Chaotu in one glorious battle! It would be fitting, don't you think?"

"Fitting? For whom?" Lijun countered. "I love my brother. He's all that I have left." She paused, the continued. "I know you lost your brother. That you're fighting for your lands. But you haven't *lost* your lands. Stripped yourself bare of any affiliation."

She gulped. "Do you know how hard it is to be lacking in any landsense? To have to struggle to pull even the slightest bit of power to yourself? To feel as though there's a glass wall surrounding you, that you can't break out of? That you're constantly trying to reach through? Then, on top of that, to know that your one consolation, the one small piece of home that you've brought with you, is constantly risking himself? And could die at any time?"

Vide nodded. "True, you've sacrificed a lot. But let's be honest here, it was to save your own lives."

Lijun smiled at him, a large, beautiful smile. "Thank you for being so honest with me," she said. "Few are, and I value that honesty more than you can know."

Vide blinked, surprised. That was…unexpected. Most woman would have flung their tea in his face. Or slapped him. He was used to that. Probably deserved it when it happened.

Someone who valued his honesty was rarer than gold in a silver mine.

"We did come here to save our own lives," Lijun

continued. "But we also hoped to help the war effort. Coming here, we had the opportunity to fight the LandHolder. We didn't have to hide anymore."

"All right," Vide said. "But that brings us back to the initial problem. How do we stop Kinaki? Sooner, rather than later?"

Lijun nodded. "We will have to build him a trap. And sweeten it with something that's irresistible to him. Chaotu and myself."

Vide found himself surprising at odds at her statement.

Yes, absolutely, put Chaotu in danger.

Yet, though he'd just met Lijun, and hadn't given her any thought as an individual outside of how he could use her, he wasn't willing to let her go, to just give her up so fast.

Like her, he'd lost so much already.

"I want to hear your plan," Vide said slowly, "how you think we can trap Kinaki. But I also want you to put some thought into how to rescue both you and your brother from being swallowed by the jaws of such a plan."

"Really?" Lijun said, the confusion making her looked even more lovely.

"Really," Vide said. He wasn't about to make any promises, particularly ones that he couldn't keep.

But for the first time since his darkest day, when he'd learned that Emil had been killed, he was finally seeing light.

Chapter Sixteen
HOUSE OF PEARL

"No," Shimokoro said adamantly.

He didn't care that he was contradicting his LandHolder. It didn't matter that he'd never stood up to Darikuto in this manner before.

All that mattered was that Darikuto listen to him, and hear reason.

They both sat at a small table in Darikuto's private tent. Not the big tent where he met with the PearlHolders. But the much smaller one, where he had private conversations and meals. The tent was divided by a colorful piece of fabric hanging from the ceiling, an ombre piece that started as the darkest blue at the top and lightened in gradual layers until it was almost white at the bottom.

Shimokoro still wore his travel clothes—plain shirt and short pants, with sturdy bamboo sandals. Darikuto hadn't been able to carry all their trunks with them on their forced march out of Yimifut's lands. Shimokoro resented losing his best formal robes. He could always have another set made, but it would cost a pretty penny to replace all the pearls that had encrusted the original.

Darikuto remained in the robes he'd worn for the ritual to take the House of Crystal lands, using his magic to keep them fresh and new looking. He always looked so much more impressive than the other LandHolders. Unnir had taken to wearing a tabard over shirt and pants, while Yimifut still dressed like a plain Holder.

"Leaving just one of those corpulent plants alive is a recipe for disaster," Shimokoro said. He wasn't yelling at Darikuto. He was just expressing himself more forcefully than he ever had before.

"But maybe I could use them. Or learn how to use them," Darikuto said, his tone wistful.

Shimokoro shuddered, unwilling to face the implications that Darikuto wasn't immediately repulsed by such things. "You cannot use them. You can only be used by them."

Darikuto nodded as if considering Shimokoro's words. "But what are they for?"

"Did you not listen to Torja when she talked of her foreseeing?" Shimokoro said. Surely the LandHolder had been paying attention. He always did. It was one of the reasons why The Plan had been so successful. Darikuto heard not just what the person was saying, but what they hadn't been saying as well. It made it so much easier to find the correct bribes or buttons to push when it came to getting people to move in the direction The Plan needed.

"I did," Darikuto said solemnly. "I'd like your opinion."

Shimokoro took a deep breath. He wasn't sure what Darikuto was after. He let all the emotion drain away, trying to regain the calm of a deep pond.

"Torja said that they were a foothold for the demons. We have long suspected that Kinaki's goal is to become the sole LandHolder. That was why after Ibitsima was killed, he attacked Unnir. If she'd been as weak as he'd thought, he would have raced across her lands and then swallowed the

House of Crystal. Then, strengthened with both their lands, he would have come for the House of Pearl next."

Shimokoro paused again, willing the emotion away, trying to speak just the facts.

"That demon who's partnered with Kinaki wants to bring the underworld to the land of the living. One of the ways to do that is to open gates between the two. The plants are a way for demons to more easily access the world of the living."

"So don't you think I could use one? Let it grow, and set a guard on it? So that when a demon arises, I could capture it?" Darikuto responded. He also didn't have any emotion in his words. It appeared to be more of an intellectual exercise for him.

"No, I do not," Shimokoro said, forcing his tone to remain even. "You do remember the false book we gave Belam, right? The one that claimed he could control the demons if he brought them forth?"

Slowly, Darikuto nodded. "I do," he said. He tilted his head to the side and looked quizzically at Shimokoro. "I'm surprised that you do."

Shimokoro shook his head. He didn't understand the question, and he didn't want to be derailed. "Everything in that book was false," he said, allowing a little more heat into his tone. "You cannot control a demon."

"But—"

"No," Shimokoro said again. "You *cannot*."

Darikuto sighed. "I suppose you're right," he said after a few moments. "I'd like to try, but as with the rest of The Plan, if I did succeed, I'd probably do it too well."

"Yes, LandHolder, you would," Shimokoro said. "The Plan has succeeded too well," he added wryly.

"Yes and no," Darikuto said. "I had believed that a little corruption might be enough to get the other LandHolders to turn against Kinaki. I hadn't anticipated what a much larger corruption might be like."

Shimokoro nodded, then added, "I don't think anyone knew. Or could know." Like Darikuto, he'd believed that just a little corruption was possible. Now, he saw that it wasn't.

"If only it could be held to just a small corner," Darikuto said. He had a longing tone to his voice that Shimokoro didn't trust. "To study it. To learn all its secrets. To steal its power."

"I understand your great thirst for knowledge," Shimokoro said. "But again, it isn't possible."

Darikuto nodded, more as a placeholder than because he appeared to agree.

"We will have to see how to get access to the girl with the ghosts," Darikuto said, abruptly changing subjects.

"Akalina?" Shimokoro said. "Maybe you can suggest that she be loaned to you, to help you contain the corruption that Torja foresaw happening in Yawatan."

He personally didn't like the girl, or want to be anywhere near her. There was an expression used in the House of Pearl about a woman who was as cold as a fish.

Akalina was one step beyond that, as if she were half-ghost herself.

"That was what I had thought," Darikuto said. "She can be part of The New Plan."

"The New Plan?" Shimokoro said. He had known that Darikuto had started work on something, he could tell by the far-away look the LandHolder's eyes took sometimes.

However, Darikuto had kept his plans very close to his chest this time, not telling any of his top advisors, at least as far as Shimokoro could tell.

"Yes," Darikuto said, nodding. "I'm still forming it. But there will be a New Plan. One that will succeed to the right extent."

Though Shimokoro was aware that those words should have filled him with pride and anticipation, he had to admit that all he felt was dread.

"Very good, LandHolder," he said. "Is there anything else?"

"No, I'll talk with you more about The New Plan later," Darikuto promised.

Shimokoro was afraid that Darikuto would do just that.

Chapter Seventeen
HOUSE OF CRYSTAL

BEFERY CAREFULLY BALANCED the tray holding the teapot and cups as she left Yimifut's tent. The night was still awfully warm outside. She missed Nyati and the cooler summers there. She'd changed into much lighter clothes—a gauzy skirt and sleeveless shirt, and merely sandals without any socks—but it was still too hot all the time. She called up a small breeze to cool herself as she made her way back to her tent.

What should she do that evening? She could finish that letter to her husband, telling him of her adventures so far. Though there wasn't much to say. She spent her days in the camp, helping when she could, cooking with the others in the evening, then making tea for the LandHolder and chatting with him for a while.

Or maybe she should—

"He's becoming dependent on you," someone said, drawing her out of her thoughts.

Menhaptu stepped out of the shadows. He was a tall, disapproving man, his pale skin and short auburn hair adding to the impression that he was always angry. He wore formal robes, of course, long and loose with pale stripes of gold—silly man thought that the outfit would bring him respect.

"What do you mean?" Befery asked, though she knew the "he" Menhaptu referred to, namely, Yimifut.

"You bring him tea and wise counsel every evening," Menhaptu said. Though Befery was tall, Menhaptu always appeared to be looking down his nose at her. "Just what do you think will happen when we get back to Nyati?"

Befery blinked, a bit taken back. "I'm hoping things go back to normal. I'll be with my family, my little ones."

Menhaptu didn't appear to expect that answer. "Won't you miss being important? Giving counsel to the LandHolder?"

Befery snorted. "You've never had children, have you? Believe me, Mommy is the most important person in the world. Until she isn't." Befery smiled at Menhaptu. "I'm just a wife and mother. I'm never going to be a member of the court, or even a person of great standing, with my own Hold."

She could see that Menhaptu wanted to object, so she held up her hand so he would let her finish.

"Yimifut is young. He needs good counsel, and counselors," Befery continued. "But he's also old, so much older than his years. If you would seek to guide him, you must first learn to listen to him."

"What are you saying?" Menhaptu said, affronted. "I listen!"

Befery managed to hold back her snort of derision this time. "Do you?" she challenged. "Do you really? You always seem to have some sort of ax to grind. Your words always come first. You talk of the people who have wronged you. Who have you helped recently?"

Menhaptu looked as shocked as if Befery had slapped him. She still pressed on.

"I know Torja has found a new way to do augury. What have you discovered?"

Finally, Menhaptu appeared to catch his breath. "We have been seeking new ways of using crystals to do foretelling," he said.

"What have you found?" Befery asked, truly interested.

Menhaptu looked to the side, as if embarrassed. Then he sighed. "It was meant as a joke," he said. "One of the acolytes suggested juggling the crystals."

Befery tried to keep her expression serious and not grin at the implications. "Were they successful?"

Menhaptu nodded. "Unfortunately. Yes. Visions appear in the space where the crystal balls are tossed into the air. At first, the visions came easily. Only ten or twenty throws would grant someone a glimpse of what was to come. As you become more accustomed to juggling, sometimes it takes close to one hundred throws before a vision is granted."

"I see," Befery said. She couldn't imagine how affronted Menhaptu must have been at the idea that some sort of performance was required for an augury.

Though wasn't that what Torja had discovered? That she had to dance, whirl until she was close to exhaustion, before she would be granted a vision?

How would visions be granted for the House of Cobalt, once Kinaki had been killed? Or even the House of Pearl? She grinned and leaned closer to Menhaptu. "Juggling isn't so bad, you know. Just imagine Shimokoro trying it."

Menhaptu couldn't help but giggle. He smiled at her, and suddenly appeared to be a much younger man. "Thank you," he said after a moment. "I see why Yimifut speaks with you."

Befery shrugged. "I do know my place," she said softly. "I'm here to help. For now. When we get back to Nyati, things will be different. I will have my family, and they will be my primary responsibility."

Menhaptu nodded. "And I know my place. Beside the LandHolder. Listening."

Befery smiled at him and proceeded on her way back to her own tent. The cool breeze she called up whirled once around the closed in area, freshening the air. Akalina wasn't there, of course. She had her own counsel to give, working with the LandHolders and their various warriors.

There wasn't much in the tent. Just two cots, one on either side, each with its own small trunk at the foot. No rugs covered the beaten down grass. They could only stand upright in the middle. The nicest thing they had as far as Befery was concerned was the lamp hanging from the center pole. She wasn't quite sure how the rock it held had been charmed, but she merely had to send a flicker of magic toward it and suddenly the interior was much brighter.

After stashing the teapot and cups under her cot, Befery sat for a while, trying to work up the enthusiasm to finish her letter. But she found herself thinking about what Menhaptu said, what he'd been implying.

If she let herself roll her eyes at the silly man, she might pull something. She wasn't some sixteen-year-old girl dreaming of meeting an Important Man. Yimifut seemed like a younger brother to her. That was all. And Befery was too practical to imagine that the LandHolder might do something foolish like try to reward her when they returned to Nyati.

No, everything was quite fine just as it was. She missed her husband, her children. And sooner or later, this war would be over, and she'd be able to go home. Put her adventures to the side, have good stories for her grandchildren.

There was nothing more important to her than that.

Chapter Eighteen
HOUSE OF COBALT

❧

WANHO KNEW that his plan to corrupt the living with seeds of demons was brilliant. He hadn't bothered to tell Kinaki about it, not until it was far too late for the LandHolder to be able to do anything about it.

The demon could tell that Kinaki was disturbed by the turn of events. He shouldn't have been. It was the natural outcome of the pair of them merging, becoming so much closer. By allowing the demon more room in his soul, Kinaki was paving the way for the underworld to be brought to the land of the living.

Wanho watched the battle that day with a sneer. Yes, the demons were losing. His warriors were being pushed back. That damned golden curtain kept advancing. He was losing his enthusiasm for the battle, as were his fighters.

However, he was leaving his own presents behind, infecting unsuspecting warriors through their blood.

If a demon had enough time, he could infect another through the air they breathed, or what they drank. But for a single exposure of two warriors fighting, it had to be a direct transfer, through the blood.

His corruption would soon spread to all the lands. Just as Kinaki had found that bedrock below the lands that connected them together, so Wanho would create his own footholds.

Every now and again, Wanho would prick Kinaki into responding, making him wade out onto the battlefield and wreak havoc with his great sword. The thrill of killing was still there. Somewhat. The glorious smells of bile, blood, and the rank odor of fear was finer than any bouquet of corpse flowers.

However, actually joining the fighting presented two problems.

One, as Kinaki's body was now so much larger than anyone else's, he stood out on the battlefield. Arrows would rain down pinging his helmet, javelins would break against his great shield, masses of warriors would swarm up, trying to overcome him.

While they weren't really in any danger of being killed, it was still annoying. It was like trying to battle a swarm of ants. Sure, he might kill masses of them. But they kept coming.

Then, there was the problem of the land itself. As Kinaki's claim on it was tenuous, his attention was constantly drawn to it, instead of paying attention to who he was fighting. They'd actually had a close call that morning, with one of taller warriors from the House of Gold actually getting close enough to slash Kinaki's arm.

Fool had died immediately, but Kinaki had also withdrawn almost immediately from the field.

Another problem, if Wanho wanted to actually acknowledge that he currently had three, and not just two, was the damned ghosts who disturbed both the living and demons alike.

The ghosts would suddenly appear in a mass behind a

group of demons, then latch on, sucking out the vitality of their prey. Eventually, the demons would realize what was happening, and would turn to destroy the ghosts. But that left them open to the attacks of the living.

The warriors who fought without the aid of a demon could also be distracted by the ghosts, who would find chinks in their armor and could freeze a body.

Directing so much power to the ghosts was draining the magic out of the land. As well as killing the ghosts. Wanho didn't need them, once he brought the underworld to the land of the living.

Kinaki, on the other hand, seemed as disturbed by the deaths of the ghosts as by his own warriors.

This war was changing the land beyond repair.

The ghosts whispered stories to Kinaki at night, when their combined body still needed to sleep. They seemed to unerringly target Kinaki's soul. Or rather, what remained of it. They made him even more uneasy about the changes Wanho had wrought.

Honestly, Wanho didn't need to be fighting Kinaki on top of everything else.

It was so much simpler down in the underworld! All Wanho had to do every day was fight. Endless battles, but still, just battles.

The living complicated things.

Wanho wasn't about to admit defeat, despite how his warriors were being pushed back.

In his heart of hearts, though, he knew that at some point, he'd have to return to the underworld. It would be difficult, returning to that dark place after having a taste of the land of the living.

But he could always take another gamble and return. Gather up armies of followers, increase his own strength and territory.

Find another fool who would open the portal between the two lands.

While Wanho didn't want to have to start again from scratch, he would. He'd do it differently the next time, find someone with less of their own will and power. Maybe start more slowly.

Eventually, he'd rule both the underworld and the land of the living. If not this time, then next.

Chapter Nineteen

HOUSE OF GOLD

AT THE END of every day, Unnir took the time to reclaim the land they'd retaken that day.

She sat in her own tent, the flap open so she could see outside. She'd left strict instructions that no one should bother her. The sun had set, and the slight coolness of the evening had begun to trickle in. Instead of wine, she preferred clear, pure water on her table, the glass pitcher refracting the lights in the tent, making it seem to sparkle.

At first, Unnir had worn formal robes in beautiful shades of green, brown, and gray, with sleeves that would brush the ground if she dropped her hands below her waist.

However, those robes had quickly become restrictive. Unnir wasn't about to go to the extremes that Torja did, wearing gauzy, flimsy material that wouldn't restrict her when she danced.

Instead, Unnir had adapted her robes into something else. She'd cut off the sleeves with joy in her heart, leaving a sleeveless tunic behind. Then she'd woven together some of that sleeve material into a badge that covered her chest.

While warriors would not wear anything under their

tunics, Unnir liked adding a lightweight shirt under hers, along with a plain skirt or trousers.

The older Holders who'd remained in Haravik would be scandalized.

Unnir found she had no sympathy for them whatsoever.

Even Yudur had approved of the changes.

As the evening settled in further, Unnir reached out with her landsense to find the current border of the lands of the House of Gold. The demarcation used to be a knife-cool edge, where her power ended and Kinaki's began, warm on his side, colder on hers.

Now, it felt as though a ragged, knotted piece of yarn had been strung between the two. It was no longer smooth or hard, but instead, jagged and prickly.

Just past her border lay the unclaimed land. Land that had at one point been hers, but that she'd relinquished in order to save her people.

Sometimes that land would be aloof, uninterested in having another Holder. That was the easiest land to take, as Unnir could just send tendrils of thought deep into the soil and draw its attention back to her.

Her hold on that land wasn't solid, but after a few days, the land would become more attuned to her again.

Then there was the land that had been corrupted by Kinaki's demons. That land had to be cleansed first before Unnir could claim it. The taint of the demons went deep, and sometimes it would take her half the night to purify it. She refreshed it as best she could, making the soil fertile again and removing the ashes.

The third type of land was the worst for Unnir to reclaim —the land that had been held for a while by the ghosts. It was almost as if the land remained haunted by its former holders. Though much of the land in the House of Gold always felt cool to Unnir as she slid her fingers through it, the haunted lands retained a soul-chilling cold.

In many ways, Unnir felt as though the land had a sense of itself, and though it didn't always welcome a Holder, it still acknowledged her.

For the haunted lands, it was as if all the souls of the ghosts who'd died that day remained in the area. The land felt fractured, not whole. Unnir tried to patch it back together as best she could, but she feared that after the battles were over, the land would never fully heal.

When she was back in Haravik, she'd feel these parts of the land like patches of rough skin on her body. Or perhaps like scar tissue, not as sensitive.

It was close to midnight by the time Unnir finished her work. However, she couldn't sleep. Not yet.

Instead, she picked up her glass of cool, clear water, drained it, and marched out of her tent.

The guards standing there stiffened.

They knew what was coming next.

At first, it was as if a cool breeze had just found them, a welcome respite from the still warm evening.

The draft grew stronger and the cold increased. A mist crept in, close to the ground at first, then rising up, as if blown by the wind.

Ghosts formed out of the fog. Generally it was only two or three, but tonight, it was just one.

Yudur.

"You have reclaimed the land, Niece?" he asked, as he always did.

"Yes, Uncle," Unnir replied. "Are you prepared for the morrow?"

"We are," Yudur said. He sighed. The sound always seemed so much sadder when coming from a ghost, filled with regret for all the things they hadn't done, or worse, had.

"You weren't my choice for LandHolder," Yudur said bluntly.

Unnir blinked, surprised. They'd danced around this landmine more than once, but Yudur had always shown her more respect than she'd thought he would have.

"I know," she finally replied.

Yudur turned to face her. He'd gone bald at a young age, and Unnir had always thought it gave him an impressive profile, the gleaming bald skull sloping down to a large, pointed nose. As a ghost, his features were less distinct, though Unnir knew better than to believe that her uncle had softened in the least. His eyebrows were still bushy though no longer black. He'd lost weight since the last time she'd seen him in the flesh, his cheeks gaunt and his jawline sharper. Thin lips seemed to retain their shape, and were still almost always twisted in a cruel smile.

"I don't know if either of my boys would have done a better job," Yudur said. "You have earned my respect."

"Thank you, Uncle," Unnir said. "That means a lot to me." She paused as the implications of what her uncle was saying sunk in.

"You won't survive, will you?" she asked.

"Maybe this battle, but certainly not the next," Yudur said. "Some ghosts are adept at seeing what lies ahead, as we are both in this world and the next. I have never pursued that. But I feel as though my body's ashes, which were scattered to the winds after I died, have returned to collect me."

Unnir had never heard of such a thing. She knew that Torja was wrestling with the problem as never before.

How did a ghost die? What happened when they did? Did they finally start their journey to the Golden Lands? Or did they just…dissolve?

No one, not even the ghosts, knew for certain.

"I will still burn incense for you," Unnir promised Yudur. "Hopefully it will ease you on your journey.

"Thank you, Niece," Yudur said. "Normally, I would tell you not to bother. I can make it on my own." He sighed again, the sound more wistful this time. "Maybe I'll see Emil this time."

"I hope you find your son in the Golden Lands," Unnir said firmly.

"That is my hope as well," Yudur said. He gave her a partial smile. "So we can go cause trouble together. Maybe become demons ourselves, sent to the underworld to test those passing through."

Unnir shivered. She wouldn't want to meet Yudur in the underworld, even if he had been her uncle.

Yudur nodded again, as if having come to a decision. "Sleep well tonight. You will need all your strength for the final push tomorrow." Then he moved off, as if he still had legs and could walk away, dissolving as he did.

Unnir felt the exhaustion from the day settle onto her shoulders, pushing her down. Yudur was right. She needed to sleep, needed to be ready in the morning.

She still paused for another moment, looking up toward the sky, at the stars partially obscured by clouds.

She wished she could see clearly. With all her soul, she longed to feel her land more cleanly as well, not this patchwork of pieces that she held together with her will as much as anything else.

If the plan worked, the battles should be over tomorrow. Kinaki would be dead, and hopefully the lands of the House of Cobalt would wisely choose another LandHolder to take the reins.

Yimifut had already come to her with a plan in case the land splintered, and would not recognize a new Holder. He didn't care about taking that land for himself.

However, they both knew that they would have to neutralize Darikuto and prevent him from grabbing any more land himself.

Unnir gave her own sad sigh. The morning was going to come all too quickly.

And, she feared, would be all too ugly.

Chapter Twenty
HOUSE OF PEARL

DARIKUTO PACED in his tent at the end of the evening. It was as sparse as the palace back in Yawatan. Plain canvas cloth to cover the grass. Pillows for kneeling on, as well as a low table for sitting at. A cot not much better than what the PearlHolders slept on. His armor hanging in the corner was the fanciest item in the whole space, and the most colorful, the steel decorated with bands of blue and black, with pearls inlaid along the collar and cuffs.

Normally, Darikuto would remain seated and let his mind do the wandering as he thought of plans, refining them, rejecting them, finding new plans.

Tonight, he felt restless, as if ocean winds propelled him back and forth while his mind desperately sought to find the answer to his conundrum.

Tomorrow, if all went well, Kinaki would be dead.

Which would mean that the lands of the House of Cobalt would be up for grabs.

No one knew if the land would immediately seek out another LandHolder, or if it would, in a fit of pique, decide to remain unclaimed.

He knew that both Yimifut and Unnir assumed that the land would seek out another Holder, choosing more wisely this time.

How could he influence the land to choose him?

Or, failing that, find some way to distract both Unnir and that damned boy Yimifut. Focus their attention somewhere else while he prepared himself and did the spell to take those lands?

The main problem with that was that the spell took time, time he just didn't have. He was certain that he could do it. He'd memorized the initial texts, but having already completed the spell once, and almost taken the lands of the House of Crystal, he knew what he'd change.

Mainly he'd add the feel of the bedrock, far below the lands themselves. He could still reach it, though it was much more difficult here than in either unclaimed land or his own lands.

The ultimate irony was that he'd had to teach both Yimifut and Unnir the trick of reaching it, in order to get to Kinaki. But he was certain that neither of them had the discipline to constantly reach for that solid rock, to force their awareness down in that manner.

Darikuto did.

He would need to focus on that underlying rock the next time he took the lands from another house.

Because he was determined that there would be another time. He would become the sole LandHolder at some point. It would be easier to do if the lands of the House of Cobalt were already in his power, but he could do it anyway.

It would take time, and much more planning. But The New Plan was shaping up nicely.

He was certain that he could isolate one of the demon plants, then use the power inherent in the flowers. Or maybe he could bind the magic the plants held, bend them to his will.

However, no one would allow him access. The plants were destroyed as soon as they were discovered. The Fevered were isolated immediately so that they couldn't infect anyone else.

Such a shame, really. Darikuto would have started to introduce prisoners to the Fevered to find out how long it took for someone else to be infected, if there were any other mitigating factors.

There was no handy collection of prisoners here, though. Any of Kinaki's warriors who were captured were killed immediately, never held and ransomed.

It seemed they carried the infection as well.

When Darikuto got back to Yawatan, he'd have the time to do his own experiments. He could control those plants, direct those seeds to grow at his will, he was certain of it, no matter what Shimokoro thought.

Finally, his distraction for the evening was announced. A guard standing at the door pulled the flap back and revealed that Akalina, the ghost girl, had arrived.

"Please, come in," Darikuto said, automatically shifting all his plans and thoughts aside so he could charm the person in front of him.

That had always been one of his greatest strengths: the ability to focus all his considerable intellect on a single problem.

This time, in the shape of a young woman.

"Thank you," Akalina said, entering the tent and looking around.

She was an odd woman, he had to admit that. She was seventeen, but she had an ethereal quality of endless childhood to her. Despite the heat, she wore her long, wavy black hair down, the front of it loosely tied back from her face with a bright blue ribbon.

Had she worn his color specifically that night? No, he recalled she'd worn it before.

Like most of the people from the House of Crystal, she wore what he would consider peasant clothes: a roughly-spun, poorly dyed maroon shirt that was sewn together out of blocks and not fitted to the body, black trousers that ended just below the knee, and straw sandals. No robes or even pretty colors.

Her face could be considered attractive, with her wide blue eyes, fine features, and pale pink lips. But she had a reserve that he hadn't been able to overcome.

Shimokoro had commented that Akalina felt like a ghost herself, removed from the immediate world.

Darikuto wasn't so sure if it was that or something else. Dark secrets that the girl held close to her chest and wouldn't ever spill, not even on her deathbed.

Darikuto indicated that Akalina should kneel on the pillows across the table from where he'd taken his own seat. A servant came in almost immediately with a tray holding two cups and an already-steeped teapot.

"Thank you," Akalina said as she accepted her cup from Darikuto. She watched him over the brim of her cup, her eyes seeking to find all his faults and secrets.

Not that she'd be able to ferret them out. Darikuto didn't share them with anyone, not even his closest advisors.

"I suppose you're wondering why I've asked you to come see me this evening," Darikuto said.

Akalina shook her head. "No, not really."

Darikuto sipped his own tea, a little surprised. Did the girl not have any imagination? "Then why do you think I have?" he finally asked.

"You want me to accompany you to the lands of the House of Pearl once we're finished here," she stated flatly.

"That's correct," Darikuto said. He immediately revised his opinion of Akalina. She was quiet and didn't speak much, but she appeared to have been watching everything that was going on. "Do you know why?"

Akalina bit her lips together for a moment before speaking. "You believe that I can help with the Fevered, back in your lands. Or at least that's what you'll tell the other LandHolders. You really just want me to talk with your ghosts."

"All of that is true," Darikuto said, impressed despite himself. He wouldn't have assumed Akalina would have guessed that much. "I would like to study your skill. To see how you communicate with the ghosts, why they are willing to listen to you."

That had always been the problem with foretelling, getting the ghosts who provided the answers to pay attention. He'd heard that the ways of augury were changing. Torja had her dancing. Menhaptu had actually learned to juggle.

He couldn't imagine what extremes Shimokoro might have to go to in order to continue telling auguries. Perhaps he'd have to start dancing naked in the rain, or cover himself in pearl paste and do cartwheels. It was certain to be something distasteful to him.

Shimokoro would do it, though, to maintain his position as the head of the Temple of Truth.

"You won't learn much," Akalina said as she put down her cup.

"Why is that?" Darikuto said, leaning in so he could not just hear her answer, but study her as she responded.

Akalina shrugged. "I've always heard the ghosts. More so than others. They sang me lullabies when I was a baby."

"Now, you see?" Darikuto said congenially. "I've already

learned something. I will only bring in those who are more sensitive to the ghosts when we start practicing."

Akalina narrowed her gaze at him, as if sensing that he wasn't completely telling the truth. "Yimifut and Unnir don't want me to go with you. You're the one who set all of this in motion. You're the one who caused Kinaki to fall, for Ibitsima to be slain. But I will go to the lands of the House of Pearl anyway."

Darikuto heard the bitterness of her words, how much she held him to blame. She honestly didn't care for him at all.

"Why?" Darikuto said, challenging. "Why would you go if you distrust me that much?" '

Akalina gave him an odd, half smile. "Because the ghosts want me to go."

With that, she stood, gave him a short half-bow, then walked out of the tent.

Darikuto knew better than to hope that meant that the ghosts were on his side, that they wanted him to succeed, to become the sole LandHolder.

Still, they wanted something from him. Otherwise, they wouldn't be sending their representative to him.

But what?

Darikuto poured himself some more tea, feeling himself relax for the first time that evening.

He had a new puzzle to solve. More plans to make.

He was certain it would all work out for him in the end.

Chapter Twenty-One
HOUSE OF CRYSTAL

AKALINA REALLY DIDN'T WANT to go to the lands of the House of Pearl. No, it was more than that. She didn't want to go anywhere with Darikuto.

However, that old ghost, Yudur, had something planned. Something that didn't bode well for Darikuto.

It was the only reason why Akalina had agreed to meet with the nasty LandHolder in the first place. She didn't like the way his eyes sucked at her, as if trying to devour her and all her secrets.

For now, though, she couldn't worry about him or whatever his plans were.

Today, they had plans of their own—a trap to capture Kinaki, and possibly end the war sooner rather than later.

Though the day was going to be warm—as all days seemed to be down here in the House of Gold lands—Akalina still put on a long white dress, similar to what she'd worn when she'd attended the court of the ghosts. Spiderweb lace covered the arms, down to her wrists, and the skirt reached her ankles. She held her hair back with a white ribbon this time. Befery had found some makeup for her, so she whitened her cheeks as well.

She debated making her lips pinker. She was officially old enough to be able to add color to her face.

She'd never had her menses, though. She never would. She was virginal, and likely to remain so. Oh, some year she might decide to take a lover. But she couldn't imagine any man would marry her, because she'd never lie about her sterile state.

She pushed those thoughts to the side. If she survived today, she'd have more than enough time to worry about the rest of her life.

Akalina left her tent, then slowly made her way to the hillside where the LandHolders had gathered.

At first, Akalina had felt awkward being among so many important people. These were the *LandHolders*. She was no longer a potential LandHolder, herself. Just someone who could speak to the ghosts.

However, Yimifut had given her a title, one unique in all the lands.

GhostHolder.

There had never been a GhostHolder before. Akalina figured that she was likely to be the last, unless the land had great need again.

She had nearly laughed at the sour expression that had crossed Menhaptu's face when he'd first heard the term. He'd blamed her for the corruption of the Chamber of Crystals, as well as the lack of ghosts in the court.

Maybe she was partially responsible for the latter, but not the former.

The LandHolders were dressed as formally as Akalina that morning. For the first time, Yimifut was in robes, long and loose. The cloth was beige, with pale stripes of red, blue, gold, and green. It reminded Akalina of the robes that

Haptomi had once worn, with the short, stiff collar and sleeves that puffed out at the shoulder and wrist.

But Yimifut looked otherworldly in his robe, particularly given how his dark curls flared out around his head like a huge halo. His pale eyes shone with magic. He gave her a quick smile before growing serious again.

Unnir wore her new tunic, done in a gray the color of storm clouds. The mass of braided green and brown ribbons in the center of her chest seemed to have a life of their own, twisting together like curly willow branches. The tunic went down to her knees, and she wore a long black skirt underneath, giving her a lot of movement, in case she decided to break into a dance, just like Torja frequently did.

Darikuito's robe resembled the armor that his warriors wore, with stripes of metal that had been wrapped in blue wire and sewn to the cloth. It fit tightly across his chest and ended mid-thigh. Pearls were encrusted along the collar and ran down the front plaques. His black trousers were also tight fitting, with more pearls and metal along the sides. They were shoved into tall black boots that seemed more appropriate for the battlefield than the hillside.

Of all the LandHolders, he looked the most severe, like a teacher who disapproved of all he saw.

Too bad Akalina didn't care what he thought.

Outside of the circle of LandHolders stood the heads of the various temples. Akalina nodded to Torja whose dress appeared to be even more gauzy than usual, showing more hints of skin. Menhaptu looked too formal in his robe, even with the three crystals he held in one hand, ready to juggle.

Shimokoro was the only one who hadn't found a new way to bring visions. Either he didn't have the imagination, or he was unwilling to bend.

She'd bet that he thought his place was secure. Darikuto might be many things, but tolerant of failure wasn't one of them. She expected Darikuto to start searching for a new head of the Temple of Truth as soon as he arrived back in the lands of the House of Pearl if Shimokoro didn't start performing soon.

The LandHolders stepped onto the cardinal points they represented: Yimifut to the north, Unnir to the east, and Darikuto to the west.

Akalina finished the circle by stepping onto the southern point. A wave of magic washed over her. She felt tied to the others with warm silken ribbons, bound together in this attempt to oust Kinaki.

Unnir led the group. "Are you ready?" she asked Yimifut, then Darikuto.

They both nodded.

"Muster your ghosts," Unnir said, turning to Akalina.

Akalina closed her eyes and reached out with her landsense. She suspected that what she called a landsense wasn't exactly what other people had, because in addition to being able to place herself on the land, she could also place where the ghosts had gathered.

Yudur had led the ghosts far into enemy territory, forming a ring just under the surface of the land. It was how they set traps for the others. By occupying an area, they could suck the magic out of it, giving themselves enough power to touch the living, as well as fight demons.

But this time, they were just gathered there, at the ready. They hadn't tried to take the land at all.

The land that the ghosts occupied would lose the touch of the LandHolder who had claimed it. All of the LandHolders understood what a distraction that was, particularly for someone like Kinaki.

Akalina opened her eyes and nodded, letting Unnir know that her ghosts were all in place. One group was concentrated in the area of the trap. Others waited just outside of that area, ready to defend the first group.

Unnir got a far-off look on her face again. "The rest are in place. We can begin."

Akalina shivered, but held her connection to the ghosts. If she needed to move them, or have them attack a different area, she'd be able to direct them.

Now, they just had to see if Kinaki would take the bait.

Chapter Twenty-Two
HOUSE OF COBALT

❧

Kinaki couldn't believe the report he was hearing.

Chaotu, his son, was calling for a personal duel with his father?

The sun was already beating down on the battlefield. To the east and to the west, some skirmishes already took place. The distant clanging of swords and shields, with the occasional cries of people dying, filled his heart with joy.

However, the center of the field was empty, ready for their individual battle.

Didn't he know that he'd lose? There was no way for a single individual, particularly one of the living, to survive a fight with what Kinaki had become.

It's a trap, Wanho warned.

Kinaki scoffed. How could it be a trap? The rest of the warriors were all to the east and west. They couldn't amass enough to take down Kinaki.

What of the ghosts?

"I will stay focused," Kinaki promised, though he had no idea if he could keep such a promise.

The ghosts could admittedly be a problem. They distracted him, and not just with their howls and warnings.

Sometimes they gave him dreams, that he didn't share with Wanho. Visions of what the past had actually been like, under a single LandHolder, so many centuries ago. Visions of what might come if Wanho ruled.

They assured Kinaki that he would fail, eventually, and the demon would come out on top. When that happened, the underworld would fill the land of the living, and nothing would ever be the same.

A part of Kinaki delighted in the corruption he saw. But there was still a small part of his soul that cried out in pain every time he realized the extent of the degradation that the land was undergoing.

The ashes that were everywhere, choking the air and the soil. The horrible vines that threatened the living and the demons alike. The way crops had failed that summer and the awful famine that was now starting to make itself known.

The LandHolders could address the latter, once they'd turned their attention away from the battles.

Wanho still wasn't certain that they should meet the challenge. He gave Kinaki full control of their shared body though, and they stepped out onto the field that had been prepared for them.

Chaotu looked so puny, standing there, all alone. He wore the armor of the House of Gold, gold and green, with flowing lines and a pointed helmet. It would be solidly protected by magic and would be able to deflect normal blows.

Kinaki's sword delivered anything but normal.

"Daddy!" Chaotu called out.

Kinaki shivered. He couldn't remember the last time his son had called him that. Possibly not since he'd been seven or eight. Formality had taken hold then. Or maybe it was the priests, teaching his children their proper place at the top of the hierarchy.

A LandHolder could no longer be "daddy" then, but merely "father." Or, as they'd grown older, "LandHolder."

"Daddy, I need to talk with you," Chaotu said, his voice so strong in the still air.

"I'd been warned this was a trap," Kinaki growled.

Wanho wanted him to strike, right now. Not give his son a chance to say anything.

The demon didn't understand about one's children, and how, no matter what, even after they'd turned against you and betrayed you by casting their allegiance with a foreign House, they still had the right to speak with their father.

With Daddy.

"Daddy, do you see the destruction all around you?" Chaotu said.

"I do, my son," Kinaki said proudly. "I have changed the world." Everywhere he looked he saw ashes. The wind always carried the faint sweet smell of corpse flowers. The taste of victory would be bittersweet, he knew, but he still yearned for it.

"Daddy, you don't really see," Chaotu said. He sounded so disappointed.

Well, that happened, Just as Kinaki was disappointed in his son, so his son felt the same way in return.

"Let me show you," Chaotu said. He raised his sword.

That appeared to be something of a signal. Before Kinaki could say anything or raise his own massive weapon, the ghosts rushed in.

Kinaki hadn't felt them before, when he'd crossed over into the cleared area. They'd been waiting, though, a thin streak of them. As they poured in on him, like an ocean wave from all sides, he felt them stripping the land he stood on of its power so that they could catch hold of him in a great net.

Then he fell, not physically, but mentally, deep inside himself, to a place that only the other LandHolders appeared to know about.

Kinaki had read about LandHolders who'd once communicated with each other from their various Holds, speaking across miles. He'd never felt the need to learn such a trick.

Seemed the others had.

He felt himself manifest in an enclosed space, surrounded by rough rock walls. Dim lights hung in the corners. A huge mantel with glowing rocks took up one wall. The air smelled of good fresh dirt, and didn't carry a hint of the ashes he'd grown so used to.

It took him a moment to realize that they were all standing on common ground as it were: the bedrock that supported all of the lands.

The others appeared in front of him, standing in their cardinal points, with him at the south. He knew Unnir and Darikuto. The stranger he assumed was Yimifut, Ibitsima's replacement.

They wore plain clothing, not robes or finery. It was as if they were four regular people, who just happened to have gathered here for a chat.

"You must stop this madness," Yimifut said. Though he was younger than the others, his voice carried reverberations of extreme age.

"The world will not survive this war," Unnir added. She, too, looked much older than he'd last remembered her.

"You need to remember your promises to protect the land, not destroy it," Darikuto said. He was the only one who looked youthful of the group, barely an adult.

Kinaki wondered how he appeared to the others. His giant body appeared to have disappeared, and in its place, just that of a tired old man.

"I don't know how," Kinaki said. He hadn't meant to say that. He pressed his fingers against his lips, as if trying to hold the words back.

"This is a place where the truth is said," Yimifut told him.

"Wanho will never relinquish power," Kinaki told them. He realized suddenly that the burden of carrying the demon had been lifted from his soul. He felt as though he could breathe deeply again, for the first time in ages.

He was not looking forward to picking up that weight again.

"Is there nothing you can do, old friend?" Darikuto said.

Kinaki looked at the other man, confused. Did he really consider them friends? Had they been at one point? He didn't remember.

"I can slow the demon," Kinaki said. "When I do, you must attack. Then I will be out of control and will strike at you with everything I have. You will only have a few moments."

The others nodded gravely to him. "We are ready."

"Goodbye," Unnir said.

Kinaki wished suddenly that he would have gotten to know the young woman, as she appeared to be turning into a fine LandHolder.

"Goodbye," Kinaki said. He paused, then before the respite was over, said quickly, "Tell my children I do still love them."

Then he was on the surface again, standing before Chaotu. Not even the blink of an eye had passed.

Had Wanho even realized what had happened? Kinaki didn't know.

He had one chance to make it right. To take the power out of the demon's hands.

He dropped his sword. It was a disgraceful act for a warrior. You always treated your weapon with dignity.

Kinaki didn't want to give Wanho any warning, however. So he left his sword lying where it was. He took a step to the side, bending his knees slightly, flowing into the first stance of the warrior exercises, the ones that had previously always put Wanho to sleep.

What are you doing?

Wanho tried to take control of the body. He sent daggers into Kinaki's joints so he cried out in pain as he bent his elbows, and howled when he took a step.

Kinaki would not stop. He did the next pose, then the next.

Wanho's efforts faded as the demon dozed.

Kinaki looked with clear eyes out over the field. The ghosts had effectively hidden the rest of the warriors from view. They surrounded him now, all poised to take him down.

He nodded to his son, understanding that it was a twisted sense of pride that permitted him to smile as his own blood took the first blow.

Then the demon came roaring back. Kinaki tried to slow down his own attack, but his control didn't last long as the demon's thoughts and despair overwhelmed him.

Kinaki fought with all his might against his attackers.

Suddenly, the ghosts emptied the claim of any LandHolder on the ground directly beneath his feet, distracting him.

It allowed the enemy time to bludgeon him further.

He still fought on, unable to help himself, feeling like a giant being swarmed by ants.

However, the ants had poison in their bite. The ghosts slipping hands up through the soles of his great war boots and onto his bare skin, sipping at his power.

Kinaki didn't see the final blow, hadn't anticipated suddenly falling on his side.

His last thought as his head was separated from his body was that finally, he could be at peace.

And the land would heal.

Then he knew nothing more.

Chapter Twenty-Three
HOUSE OF GOLD

CHAOTU TOLD himself that he didn't care if he survived the battle with Kinaki, or rather, that *thing* that his father had turned into.

He was lying to himself, though. He very much wanted to survive.

He still went out onto the battlefield alone, without any men around him. His only backup was Lijun. She would have come out next if Kinaki had turned away, hadn't stepped forward into the trap.

The sun beat down fiercely on his peaked helmet—so very different from the flat-topped, boxy helmets that warriors from the House of Cobalt generally wore. Fighting continued off in the distance, to either side of him. No birds sang. The constant buzzing of flies feeding off the dead remained.

He couldn't say for certain if he felt the line when he crossed it, that demarcation that the ghosts had drawn, deep under the soil. Perhaps it was just his fear that made him shiver as he strode forward.

No warriors from the House of Cobalt accosted him. The

challenge had already been issued and accepted. They still sneered at him. Who was he, merely one of the living, to challenge their LandHolder, who was already on his way to becoming a god?

Chaotu had heard the rumors before he'd left the House of Cobalt lands. The LandHolder was becoming so much greater than he had been. He commanded demons and the living. Surely that meant he was transforming into something greater than both?

No, Chaotu decided as that *thing* swaggered out to meet him.

He didn't know for certain what his father had become. However, it was no god.

It was an abomination.

It had grown several feet taller than any of the living. In addition, Kinaki's face was starting to push out, as if the weight of his great flat helmet was too much. He had more of a snout now. When he spoke, Chaotu could see that the tips of his incisors had grown longer, becoming fangs. The gloves Kinaki used had long claws at the tip of each finger. Chaotu didn't know if those were part of the glove or growing from Kinaki's fingertips.

Chaotu used the words that Vide had suggested, calling to what remained of Kinaki's soul. He didn't allow the tears to run down his cheeks when he used the word, "Daddy."

He was playing a part. Nothing more. He was not a young boy crying out for his father.

He might have been lying about that as well.

He couldn't believe it when Kinaki started doing the warrior exercises that Chaotu and every other warrior practiced religiously.

Something was wrong. Kinaki's face was contorted with pain, despite how fluidly he flowed from one position to the next. He howled and cried out, but Chaotu couldn't see what was attacking Kinaki.

Unless it was from within, the demon fighting for control.

While the movements finally smoothed out, Kinaki's howls subsided. He nodded toward Chaotu, a look of… something flowing across his face.

Pride? Joy? The expression seemed alien on the mien of whatever it was that his father had become.

Chaotu took it as a signal, however, and charged forward, striking the first blow, a solid hit to Kinaki's knee, sending it sideways and making the monster standing before him stagger.

With an ear-shattering roar, Kinaki dove for his sword, swinging it with blinding speed at Chaotu's head.

Though Kinaki had grown to such a huge height, he hadn't fought very much in his new form.

He easily missed when Chaotu ducked.

A large group of warriors rushed in, while a second group stayed behind, guarding the backs of the first group, not allowing any support to reach Kinaki, keeping the LandHolder isolated on the battlefield.

Chaotu and the others concentrated their blows on Kinaki's legs. More than one of those bravely attacking the LandHolder were killed.

However, Chaotu took his opening when he saw it, skewering Kinaki's knee, the one he'd first struck.

Kinaki could no longer support his massive weight on that leg, and fell to his side, a look of surprise on his face.

Darikuto's primary PearlHolder, Chuyoko, surged forward. With a single blow of her great sword, she cut off Kinaki's head.

A massive gust of wind blew out from the body, forcing Chaotu to stagger backwards a few steps.

It flattened many of the warriors from the House of Cobalt. Except, they didn't get back up again. The wind had carried the demons away, leaving rotting husks behind.

Those of the living who'd been fighting without a demon continued to fight on, desperate now. They killed themselves rather than surrender.

Chaotu stood alone again in the middle of the battlefield as the last of the battle roared around him. He didn't mourn his father—Kinaki hadn't been that for quite some time.

No, he mourned the Land. He'd felt it passing out of the former LandHolder.

For a brief moment, he'd hoped that maybe, *maybe*, the Land would settle on his shoulders, choosing him even though he'd turned his back on it.

However, he'd felt it flow away, toward the south, where an old woman warrior still fought to keep her Hold separate and clean from the horrors that had crept in.

She would come to see them all soon. Or rather, the other LandHolders.

The lands of the House of Cobalt were no longer his concern.

Now, he had to see if he could make a new life in the lands of the House of Gold.

Chapter Twenty-Four
HOUSE OF PEARL

CHUYOKO RAISED her glass again as another round of congratulations went through the feasting tent, with everyone praising the warriors and each other for finishing the battle, for defeating Kinaki, and for her, in particular, for striking the killing blow.

None of these idiots had to know that her cup was filled with water, not wine. And they didn't seem to understand that they hadn't fully won. Not yet. There was still work to be done, battles to be had.

The land still needed to be cleansed. While most of the demons had been wiped out, they'd left their spoor behind, which carried the seeds of further destruction.

Every one of those damned vines needed to be uprooted and torn out, burned in white hot fire. Possibly the earth needed to be salted as well, at least in some places.

Fakra, the new LandHolder for the House of Cobalt, was going to have to completely rebuild Jinyi. The other LandHolders had pledged their support for her efforts. Particularly when Fakra immediately re-established the northern border for the House of Cobalt lands to the old line, giving all of the new acquired territory back to the House of Gold.

Though Chuyoko had only met Fakra in passing, she already had a deep respect for the other woman, who'd evidently been a warrior for Kinaki, back before he'd been infected with a demon. She'd been managing a Hold, waging a continual battle to keep her land clean.

Fakra had been as surprised as everyone else that the Land had chosen her. However, she'd joked that just meant no rest, merely more battles on a bigger scale, and she was used to fighting.

Chuyoko suspected that she understood Fakra's sentiment more than any of the others.

Darikuto's questions had disturbed Chuyoko, more than she cared to admit. Her LandHolder was determined to keep some of the demon plants around, certain that he could contain them.

Chuyoko wasn't used to questioning her LandHolder. He'd always seemed so wise to her, able to plan out further than anyone she'd ever known. He held so much knowledge in his head.

However, the pursuit of more knowledge, particularly of the demons, seemed like folly at best.

Chuyoko remained in the feasting tents for a short while before slipping away into the darkness of the night beyond the brightly lighted area. She stopped just outside the tents, still listening to the revelry but no longer a part of it.

The air was still too warm. Chuyoko was looking forward to being back in Yawatan, with the ocean breezes and the heavy mists. Stars lit the dark sky, a welcome light. She paused, letting her eyes grow accustomed to the dimness.

Another shape took place just beside her. It took Chuyoko a few moments to realize that Fakra stood there, also breathing in the peace of the night.

Another rousing cheer cut through the quiet. Chuyoko shared a grimace with the other woman.

"They don't understand how much battle is ahead," the older warrior said.

"Aye, they don't," Chuyoko said grimly.

"You do, though," Fakra said. "The cleansing of the land must be your first priority."

"It will be," Chuyoko said. Though she didn't really know the other woman, she trusted her instinctively, as a warrior would trust a PearlHolder.

"No matter what the wishes of your LandHolder may be," Farka continued as if Chuyoko hadn't said anything.

Chuyoko sighed. She was afraid that was going to be the crux of it. Darikuto and his plans that went too well.

"He cannot be allowed to keep any of the vines or plants, or even the seeds from the demons," Fakra said. "Or we will be back exactly where we started, all of the land slowly being corrupted until the underworld is brought into the land of the living."

"I understand," Chuyoko said. And she did. She didn't want to admit it, but Darikuto, in his insistence on being able to isolate some of the awful plants, was wrong.

"You must stop him," Fakra said. Her words sounded like orders from a grand BlackPearl Holder.

Or possibly from the Goddess Morta herself.

"No matter what the cost."

Chuyoko gave the other woman a grim smile. That appeared to be the most popular phrase of these times. To do what needed doing.

No matter the cost.

Chapter Twenty-Five
HOUSE OF CRYSTAL

YIMIFUT TOOK Befery's advice and planned on only taking a few of his advisors and warriors with him back to the lands of the House of Crystal.

There was still Darikuto to settle, but Yimifut needed to see to his land first.

Unnir would take care of the rest of his people, all his warriors, speed them across her lands.

However, it would take them a week to do what Yimifut was determined to do in a single day.

He couldn't admit to anyone, not even to Befery, how much his soul longed for his land, how he'd awaken in the morning with his cheeks wet from tears he'd shed through the night. It had only been a few days, but it felt like a few lifetimes.

But would she take him back?

While most LandHolders didn't think of their lands in terms of a gender, he knew that for him, the lands of the House of Crystal were definitely female. She was as cool and clear as a winter morning, possessing the stillness that only comes just before it starts to snow. In her heart was the heat of a hearth fire, warming his soul. She laughed like the burbling streams, and her anger was dark and terrible, like woods gone wild.

Yimifut had gathered all the people he'd take with him just outside of his tent. He'd already said his goodbyes to the other LandHolders. The dawn had come, the air warming quickly. At least the smell of ash was gone, though it would take Unnir a long time to heal her land.

Befery smiled at Yimifut as he waited. Maybe she knew why he hesitated. They'd spoken of it before. She nodded to him, as if to assure him that it was going to be fine.

Yimifut took a deep breath, reaching down to the bedrock that lay beneath all the lands. He had been astonished when Darikuto had shown it to him and Unnir, as part of their trap for Kinaki.

Darikuto must have been desperate for him to reveal such power.

Yimifut understood why Darikuto had found the bedrock in the first place. The LandHolder was still determined to force the others out, to become the sole LandHolder of all the lands.

The power to do that lay in the bedrock.

Torja and Menhaptu had insisted that they find the common ground between all the LandHolders. It had taken them a couple of days to figure out what that meant, the land that supported all of them.

Only after they'd pondered the meaning of the foretelling for a day or more did Darikuto step forward and show the other LandHolders the bedrock, and the trick of accessing it.

It had been easiest for Unnir, as they were in her lands. Yimifut had quickly figured it out, though.

He'd have to see how easy or difficult it would be back in his own lands.

There was no more delaying. No reason why he shouldn't

just leave. With a sigh, Yimifut reached out and *under*, seeking his way with his landsense, until he found the edges of his reach.

Then he took a step forward, onto that spot, pulling the group who was with him along.

He stopped and took another deep breath. Behind him, he could no longer see where Unnir and her warriors waited.

One step. Many miles.

Then he did it again.

❀

As Yimifut had suspected, it took most of the day for him to cross the lands of the House of Gold. The day had started out too warm, but as they progressed north, had grown noticeably cooler. The sun stayed bright in the sky, no clouds to mar the incredible blue. The smell of baked earth and dry grasses filled the air. Soft breezes sprang up as they progressed, teasingly familiar.

The border between the House of Gold and the House of Crystal was not obvious to the casual observer. There were no sudden hills or valleys. The land remained flat.

But Yimifut still felt it, just over there. It was as welcome as dipping your toes in a cool stream on a hot day. He felt drawn to it, his mouth watering in anticipation of that first clean, cool bite of sweetened, shaved ice.

At the same time, he hesitated. This was it. The final step. The time to see if the land would take him back, after he'd left her.

"It will be fine," Befery said to him.

Yimifut started. He hadn't heard her come up beside him.

"I know," he said. "But still…"

"You will make it work," Befery said. "I believe in you.

You are our LandHolder. The land chose you. It will accept you again."

Yimifut sighed. "I know you're right." But he still didn't move.

Befery rolled her eyes at him. "Sometimes it's easy to forget that you're still a teenager. Just do it."

"All right," Yimifut said, stung. It was the first time that Befery had ever referred to his age. He'd gotten used to thinking of them as peers.

He grabbed his people roughly together and took that last step, across the border, to his home.

It was like jumping headfirst into a cool pond. The shock of it stole his breath away. All his senses were overwhelmed. The taste of cold snow filled his mouth, roaring streams were all he could hear, his eyes saw the whiteness of the mountains, and the smell of good, fresh soil surrounded him.

At first, he struggled to find himself, shaking his physical head that was so far away, almost as if it floated somewhere far above him, like a bird tied to a string.

Soothing hands touched his shoulders. Befery, he realized. His head was in her lap. He must have fallen.

He knew he couldn't go back to his body. Not yet. He had to delve further into the land first.

His body was safe.

Yimifut turned and dove further into the heart of his mistress, that cool lady who both welcomed him as well as overwhelmed him, demanding everything from him.

He swam through her rivers, buoyed up by his adoration of her. Climbed naked up her steepest mountains, protected from her cold by his lack of fear. Plummeted into the depths of her mines, the heart of her crystal, encased by his awe of her.

No matter where she took him, he met her with love and courage.

Finally, they seemed to reach an accord. It felt as though the land curled up on his side, wrapped around him like a lover, but no longer completely encasing him. He found his hands wandering her skin, reaching for mountains and valleys alike.

Never again, he promised her, allowing her cold breath into his mouth, like a shared, frozen kiss.

That seemed to settle her, and she draped herself around him, like the cloak he'd first felt.

He knew that he still had work to do. That there were parts of the land that felt frozen to him, as if his landsense couldn't reach fully into those areas.

Some of those were to the west, where he'd fought Darikuto. The ghosts had swallowed up the magic of the land, stealing his claim on it.

However, he was aware those weren't the only patches. He'd spend years seeking them out, soothing them, trying to win them back over.

He'd fail, he knew. The land was never going to be fully his again. She had too much of her own awareness, now.

And possibly that was for the better. Only a strong LandHolder would be able to hold on to her. Someone dedicated to her, and her alone.

Darikuto would never succeed in his attempt to rule over all the lands as a single LandHolder.

Yimifut felt himself surfacing, felt his own body return to him.

He'd been right—he was lying flat on his back, with his head in Befery's lap.

"Are you all right?" she asked when he opened his eyes.

"I am," he said. "Thank you for protecting me."

"I knew you had work to do," Befery said. "I wouldn't allow anyone to disturb you."

Yimifut turned his head. Guards stood in a circle around

him. Just beyond them stood Menhaptu and the other heads of the temples.

What would they have done had they been able to reach him? Disturb him, that was for certain. Try to wake him up, make him return to his body.

They would have destroyed whatever connect he'd been able to establish with the land.

"Thank you," Yimifut said again.

Befery gave him a proud smile, like that of a mother to a son. "I knew you could do it. The land feels more settled now."

"I'll have to go on more promenades than the previous LandHolders," Yimifut said as he sat up. "Once a year isn't going to be enough." He stood up, then offered his hand to Befery so she could stand as well.

"I will go with you only once a year," she announced.

Yimifut grinned. That seemed like the perfect solution for what he was going to do without Befery to give him advice regularly.

Oh, they'd still have tea together. He'd make sure of that.

But once a year, he'd be able to listen to her wisdom without the rest of the court around.

"Let's go home," Yimifut announced to the rest of the people waiting for him.

It was time.

Chapter Twenty-Six

HOUSE OF COBALT

❦

YADAI, the newly elected head of the Temple of Truth, stood at the doorway of her temple and looked around.

Or rather, where the new Temple of Truth would be.

The old temple had been razed to the ground, as had so many buildings in Jinyi. They'd either fallen of their own accord with the passing of Kinaki, or, when the true nature of their structure had been revealed, been burned.

Yadai would never forget how the scales had fallen from her eyes and she'd suddenly seen the truth of everything, how the walls were supported by writhing vines, the gaping holes in all the roads that were filled with a disgusting morass of an unknowable nature, empty wooden cages in the courtyards put together with tar and sticky vines that had supposedly held ghosts at one point, and the stench of those hideous flowers that still bloomed everywhere.

In addition to tearing down the building, Fakra had filled the underground chamber where Belam had first encountered the demons.

Yadai planned on reorienting the temple, so that the filled in area was directly underneath the altar of the God

Djediese. She could see it in her mind, how he'd sit on his throne, with a great rainbow cloak flowing out on both sides of him.

The rainbow had been what had finally given her a clue about how those in the House of Cobalt would start to do auguries again. Certain types of metal that had been heated with flame would change colors, sometimes turning into a rainbow. The mines of the House of Cobalt were famous not merely for their minerals but also for their coal and metals.

After some experimenting, Yadai had figured out how thin to make the metal so that it rang with a clear note when she struck it with a cloth covered hammer. The steel drums that carried the best tune were also the ones with the greatest range of colors.

Making music as well as dancing behind her drums granted her the visions that she needed as the head of the Temple of Truth. She carried those drums with her all the time now, strung to her back like a backwards set of breasts.

She was just lucky she didn't have to sing, unlike that poor bastard Shimokoro, who had a beautiful speaking voice but didn't appear to be able to carry a tune worth a damn.

The temple she'd have the LandHolder raise up would have a vaulted ceiling. That way, the notes would have space to rise up. She could see all the people who would come to attend an augury standing and dancing as well.

That was one of the biggest changes that had occurred. Foretelling was no longer done in secret chambers, deep under the earth, but instead, in front of an audience who would carry the word of what was learned.

Yadai walked from where she envisioned the entrance of the temple would be to the heart of it, standing on the altar space, then turning and looking back out. Right now, she saw the ruined garden to her left, all the plants burned and many patches of earth salted. To her right stood one of the repaired streets. Those had been the first thing that Fakra had worked on. People could sleep in tents. However, they had to have access to fresh food and water, which meant roads.

The temple wouldn't be anywhere near as grand as it once had been. Yadai understood why. Belam had caused so much grief, it was surprising that Fakra had agreed to having a Temple of Truth at all.

However, she wouldn't allow people to shift all the blame to the priest. Yes, he'd been partially responsible.

But most of the fault lay with Kinaki.

Yadai took a deep breath. She felt the spirit fill her.

She never knew when the need for finding a vision would overcome her. Sometimes she woke from a sound sleep and found herself banging on her drums before her eyes fully opened. Other times, she would have to leave a meal, or even the occasional meeting, just so she could go play.

Honestly, she hadn't ever used it as an excuse to get out of talking with some of the old farts from the other temples. Really.

She pulled the drums from her back. A set of cleverly hinged sticks that she wore at her waist, hanging down like a sword, practically assembled themselves, providing her with a platform on which she could place her drums.

Her hammers felt right in her hands, the weight of them grounding her as the song took her.

Yadai began to play, softly at first, then loudly enough to ring the heavens. People who were going along the road, minding their own business, stopped to listen. Some were captured by her tune, and joined her in the newly assigned temple space, their own passion making their feet move as they lifted their voices in joyful noise.

Yadai smiled and nodded her encouragement as the vision of what this place would be like filled her.

No walls could hold that vaulted roof. The new temple

would always be open, so that those who needed to hear could join her at will. No pews or seats. Just the statue of the God Djediese behind her, and a chorus of singers beside her.

The dancing of feet consecrated the space, marking it as holy. No matter what other ceremonies would be held, Yadai knew that this one was the most important of all.

It would take time, and more than just dancing and singing, to cleanse Jinyi and the rest of the lands of the House of Cobalt. Plus, there was still Darikuto to deal with.

However, for the first time, Yadai felt hope that it would happen in her lifetime.

Chapter Twenty-Seven

HOUSE OF GOLD

❧

TORJA DREAMED OF FRACTURED LAND.

At first, everything was fine, as it generally was in dreams.

But then, fissures started to appear. First, in the streets of Haravik. Tiny seams would appear in the center of the busy streets, subtle at first, just a thread, but growing day by day. Children dared each other to leap over the gaping holes. Adults sensibly walked around them.

Then the cracks started to form in the palace itself. The throne room halved, then quartered, then continued to splinter until it seemed as though each Holder who visited Unnir had their own separate island to stand on.

However, as was the nature of dreams, Torja didn't see anything wrong. It was just one more thing to grow accustomed to in the new lands of the House of Gold.

Like the lack of ghosts. Or the diminished magic. Or even the slowly changing appearance of the people, as the other Holders began to follow Unnir's lead, ditching their formal robes for new tunics and badges.

The fissures didn't become critical until they reached the

mines. The MineHolder's guild implored the LandHolder to come and help.

For some reason Torja couldn't quite discern, Unnir sent her instead.

They climbed the foothills to the east slowly, scrambling over sun-kissed rocks, the smell of heather sweet in the air.

Until finally they reached their destination.

The devastation of the area took Torja's breath away. Instead of small cracks or even crevices, there were huge gaping holes where the mines had once stood. Instead of a series of elegantly looping tunnels—that echoed the braided badges that most people now wore—the land had been laid open with all her wealth exposed.

Torja felt devastated, as if she were seeing the aftermath of incredible violence and rape. She wanted to recover the earth herself, hide its scars.

But all Torja could do was dance for the ghosts and those around her, dance to hide her shame and the shame of the land, dance while her tears streamed down her face and her sobs rose up.

When Torja awoke, she was as exhausted as if she'd spent all that time climbing the mountains and dancing for the gods.

She gulped down the water waiting her on her bedside table, then drew her knees up and rested her head on them, her arms wrapped tightly around herself, as if possibly she could draw some comfort from her own covered shape.

Once Torja recovered, she knew that she was going to have to dance some more, to see if she could tease out what the meaning of the dream had been.

Because those fissures, those cracks, were coming. And unless Unnir and the others were prepared, they would be overwhelmed.

TORJA WASN'T surprised when her vision brought her to Vide's door. The war had changed the man considerably. Whereas before he'd never held his tongue, always lashing out with the cruelest and most sarcastic remarks, now he was almost a ghost of himself. He might still smile sardonically, but he stayed silent.

What did surprise her was that when she knocked on the door, Lijun answered it.

The other woman looked her over, wearing a secret smile. Her long black hair was held up with elegant long sticks, tendrils dangling and slightly curled. The badge on her tunic had more black and red ribbons on it than most, the colors of her former house.

"Let me know if you need anything else," Lijun said over her shoulder to Vide, who stood by his open window.

Vide just nodded, then his eyes returned to Torja. "Come in," he said in a mild voice that just sounded wrong.

As soon as the door shut behind Lijun, Vide asked, "What dire new prophesy do you have for us today?"

Torja kept her smile to herself. That sounded a lot more like the Vide of old. Perhaps he was finally healing from the death of his brother.

And what did Lijun have to do with that?

She pushed aside her speculation. "Cracks," she said. "Fissures. Something breaking apart. And we have to be ready for it. But I can't figure out what is going to break."

Vide tilted his head to one side. "Can't you really?" he asked. "It's obvious."

When he told her, Torja found herself nodding. Yes, he was right. It was fairly obvious.

Fortunately, he also had already started making plans on what to do next.

Chapter Twenty-Eight
HOUSE OF PEARL

❧

OF COURSE, the new path to augury would be one that Shimokoro struggled with. Instead of elegantly watching a scene in a reflective pond, now he had to sing to the damned water. Not some set tune, either. He could tell when the water grew restless, and he needed to change it up.

Honestly, he felt like a performing mountebank. However, Shimokoro was aware that while Darikuto would allow Shimokoro to keep his office, the LandHolder would start agitating if the head of the Temple of Truth couldn't perform a simple augury. Particularly now that Kinaki was gone and the lands of the House of Cobalt were starting to be cleaned up.

Except…the demons weren't gone. Shimokoro knew that without even the most basic of auguries.

The house of the spy Benitoyo had dissolved into a writhing mass of vines and stinking corpse flowers. Because no one understood what was happening, the plants and disease had spread through half the city.

Back in the House of Gold, the Fevered had been

immediately isolated, and frequently killed before they became a walking, sprouting disease, able to infect others.

Darikuto insisted that his guards move more cautiously. It was one thing to offer a clean death to a warrior. It was something completely different to start killing civilians.

So the infection spread.

Darikuto claimed that it was all going well, according to The New Plan.

Shimokoro had his doubts.

In Shimokoro's worst nightmares, Kinaki came back and walked the streets of Yawatan at night. The giant demon infected people by the hundreds, breathing out a reeking miasma that mingled with the sea fog.

That morning, Shimokoro sat in his office in the Temple of Truth, humming at a shallow bowl of water sitting on his desk. The beautifully made bowl was polished silver, two palm-widths across at the widest point of the oval.

The water stayed calm, as if listening raptly. Shimokoro was well aware that he didn't have much of a singing voice. He'd started taking lessons every morning, practicing things he'd never even known had existed before this, like scales and half notes. He was determined to master this new form of augury, though.

He didn't want to be pushed to the side. He wanted to stay central to The New Plan.

Even if he didn't much care for the details, such as exposing prisoners to the Fevered to see how long it took for them to be infected.

Fakra was working diligently on cleaning out the lands of the House of Cobalt. Shimokoro was concerned that Darikuto didn't appear to be working as hard to clear the demons and their spawn out.

So that morning, he'd decided to cast a small augury. He knew he needed to work with the water every day, as well as his voice. While he understood that most auguries now were performed in public, that still didn't sit well with him.

He longed for quiet caves and silvered water.

His office was hardly appropriate for an augury, and barely comfortable any more. The leather-bound tomes that lined the shelves didn't contain any wisdom for dealing with his current situation. A fine mosaic of waves and water covered the floor and seemed to hold in the cold of the morning marine layer. Even his desk felt too big for the space, a barrier to the truth instead of a bulwark to shelter him.

Shimokoro persisted. He changed his tune, hopping up and down a scale, skipping notes, while adding in a few trills.

That made the water happier. It started to shiver, as if a wind caressed the surface.

Though Shimokoro would have preferred a set tune, or even a specific hymn to sing, none of that worked. He had to find music inside of himself, sing nonsense syllables and a tune of his own making.

He was earnest about it, though well aware that he wasn't artful. The diligence he practiced with as well as his sincerity counted, though.

Finally the water splashed on its own, as if a pebble had been dropped in the center of it.

Shimokoro continued to pour out his tune, his question already formed in his mind.

What will happen to Darikuto next?

He knew that the question was too open ended. The waters could show Darikuto having breakfast after getting out of his bed, or even going to sleep after a long day's work.

But there was also a chance that the waters would show Shimokoro something important.

He shivered as the surface of the water grew as silver as

the bowl it lay in. Instead of reflecting his face like a mirror, he saw Darikuto's face.

The LandHolder was down in the prison underneath the palace, watching one of the Fevered. The man was dying. His clothes had been stripped from him, and the all-too-familiar sight of something crawling under his skin was evident.

He called out something—a name, perhaps? It caught Darikuto's attention, and he took a step forward.

Shimokoro called out a warning, but it was too late.

The Fevered man's belly exploded outward with a horrible squelching sound, or possibly that was just Shimokoro's imagination. Seeds flew everywhere, wiggling on their own accord, seeking fertile ground to dive into and spread their corruption. Vines spewed out like flying snakes, striking everywhere.

One landed solidly on Darikuto's throat.

The vision from the mirror actually had no sound, just the horrific images of Darikuto's face contorting with pain as it grew darker, the way he pulled at the horrible vine wrapping around his throat to no avail, how the LandHolder fell to his knees.

But that wasn't the worst part.

No, it was when Darikuto rose again, his eyes grown dark and soulless. He appeared to be searching for something.

More snakes to swallow? More seeds to cast?

Shimokoro didn't want to see any more. His hand of its own accord splashed down into the bowl, before Darikuto's horrible eyes sought out the spot from which Shimokoro watched.

Could he see across time and space, catch who was spying on him?

Shimokoro had never heard of such a thing.

Then again, he'd never seen such magic before, either.

As Shimokoro dried his hand, he stared out across his office.

He knew there was no way to reason with the LandHolder. Darikuto thought himself invulnerable. He would continue with his experiments. Even if Shimokoro managed to prevent this particular infection, there would be others.

Demons of the underworld would try to take over the lands of the living again.

Only this time, they might succeed, with Darikuto leading them.

There was only one person who Shimokoro could talk with about this.

It might cost him his life. But it was either that, or the death of all of the lands.

He paused, laughing at himself.

He'd always wanted to be part of something bigger. Always known that he'd been born for greatness.

He'd just never imagined it would be anything like this.

Chapter Twenty-Nine
HOUSE OF CRYSTAL

❧❧

Akalina would never forget her first night in Yawatan.

First, there was the palace. It was such a foreign place for her. Instead of comfortable wood, brick, and stone, she would swear that at least half the walls were made out of paper. Everything was painted, and it all felt artificial. Even the gardens were manicured within an inch of their lives, instead of letting wild things grow.

Her bed was comfortable enough, though the mattress wasn't stuffed as well as hers was at home. The room itself was a pale green that she supposed was meant to be soothing, but it looked too much like mold to her. Guards stood outside her door, supposedly there to fetch her anything she wanted, though she suspected they were also there to keep her inside her room, at least until dawn.

She could always sneak out the window, despite being on the second floor. Her magic would break her fall. But then what? She couldn't just leave. She needed to stay here, in the lands of the House of Pearl, and do the bidding of the ghosts.

One of the things that she'd first asked for had been a small brazier for incense. Of course, the one that Darikuto had had delivered was made out of silver filigree, expensive and delicate. Akalina was afraid she'd break the damned thing just by lifting it up.

She wasn't familiar with the incense that he'd sent along with it. Instead of a type of resin, it had been reduced to a fine powder, then pressed back together in a cone shape.

At least it smelled good, sweet like jasmine.

Akalina dimmed the lighted rocks in the corners of her room, then set a spark to the incense. The smoke rose up straight, in a tall column. Then the top of it mushroomed out, forming a huge disc. It kept expanding, until most of the ceiling was covered in rolling smoke.

Yudur dropped down from the morass. "The lines have formed well," he said cryptically.

Akalina merely nodded, as if she understood what he was talking about. Communicating with the ghosts was frequently like that. Made her roll her eyes more often than not.

"The demons have a larger foothold here than we'd anticipated," he added.

Akalina shivered. She wasn't completely surprised, not given how Darikuto talked about them. He didn't understand the danger he was in.

"Tonight, I need you to lead us to the heart of the infection," Yudur directed.

Akalina felt herself pale. "What do you mean?" she asked. She'd always just assumed the ghosts could go wherever they wanted to. They were ghosts, right? No physical body?

"You need to take us to where the infection started," Yudur stated. "You need to help root us there."

"Now?" Akalina asked. It had been a long day of travel, though Akalina had to admit that Darikuto did carry his people more smoothly than Yimifut had. She suspected it was a learned thing, as her LandHolder was still so new to everything.

But it might also have been a Darikuto thing. That LandHolder loved to show off, trying to give the impression that he was better than everyone else.

"Yes. Now," Yudur said.

"But the guards—"

"We will hide you from them," Yudur assured her.

Akalina sighed. It really didn't matter how tired she was, or how her heart ached to be back home, snuggled in among the roots of the mountains back in Nyati. Or how Darikuto still gave her the creeps with his smug smile and greedy eyes.

She had no idea what she'd do after this, so she had no life to look forward to, no expectations.

Anything but traveling with the ghosts trailing behind her, like a cold veil.

As Yimifut had joked once, the motto of the House of Crystal while he was LandHolder might be, "Whatever it takes."

Akalina nodded to Yudur. At least she hadn't changed into her sleeping gown yet, but still wore her travel clothes: a sturdy maroon blouse and black trousers that ended just below her knee, with straw sandals.

She'd seen Darikuto giving her a snide look, as if what she wore wasn't good enough for him.

Too bad.

Yudur pulled more ghosts out of the clouds that still covered the ceiling of her room. Akalina recognized some of them—Mitolina, the great warrior from the House of Crystal, who still wore her armor, even after death, Hapta, a poet from the House of Cobalt, and even Junikito, the GuildHolder for the armor makers from the House of Pearl.

The ghosts formed a circle around Akalina, like a great wet shroud. She'd trained herself to see through them, having grown used to their form. They just added a white glaze to the world when she unfocused her eyes a bit.

Yudur passed through the door while the others waited. Akalina heard the signal with her companions, a whistle of all's clear.

Akalina pulled the door open and slipped through.

The attention of the guards was firmly fixed on a spot on the wall to the right of the hallway. Akalina didn't know what Yudur was showing them. Naked girls perhaps, knowing the old LandHolder's tendencies.

Akalina slipped down the hallway as silently as the rest of the ghosts. She felt more trailing after her, a silent wake. Only the most sensitive would feel their passing, a cold wind blowing against the normal currents of the night.

The ghosts led her to a back corridor, and outside the palace through an unmarked door. The stars were bright points against the black sky. The air felt soft against her cheeks, and in the distance, she thought she heard ocean waves.

Tomorrow, maybe she'd actually get the chance to see the water.

Tonight, there was work to be done.

AKALINA LED the ghosts as best she could, using her landsense in this foreign place to guide her. She wasn't exactly certain why they couldn't find this place themselves. Maybe the whole city was infected with demons, and they couldn't pinpoint the source?

While the ghosts generally felt cold to her, the demons had always felt warm, with their ashes and their fires.

That was the sense that she focused on as they made their

way through empty streets toward the area that felt warmest to her.

Not a cozy warmth, like heated stones in a hearth on a winter's day. No, more like the stifling heat of a smithy, where weapons were forged.

She smelled the place before she saw it. She stopped and coughed, almost gagging on the too-familiar odor of corpse flowers and ashes.

Yudur turned back to look at her, disappointment obvious in his face. "Come on," he said impatiently.

Akalina nodded, trying to catch her breath.

A ghostly hand covered her nose and mouth. Through the cool wetness, she could finally breathe. She nodded her thanks to Hapta and started walking again.

The sight around the next corner made her stop again.

Instead of low houses with wooden walls, a three-story structure reared up. The thing spread out for half a block, taking up what had probably been five or six houses.

A mass of vines made up the walls. They undulated slowly, as if dancing to a tune she couldn't hear. Blue cornflowers with rotten hearts lined the edges of the structure. Sharp stakes shot up close to the walls, like a barricade, to stop anyone from storming the building. Through the ghost hand on her mouth, Akalina could still taste ashes. Despite the heat, she shivered, the grotesque nature of the thing in front of her frightening.

Why hadn't Darikuto come here directly and torn this thing down? Ousted it from the lands of the House of Pearl?

It shouldn't be allowed to live. Not here.

No guards stood at the edges of the thing. Now that Akalina looked more closely, she saw that some sort of magical shield was placed around it.

Did Darikuto really believe that was enough to protect him?

Probably. He didn't care if anyone else got infected by passing spores.

"We need to get to the heart of that thing," Yudur said grimly.

"You want me to go in there?" Akalina asked, horrified.

"Yes," Yudur said.

Fear rooted Akalina in place. There was no way she enter that place and not be infected. She'd become one of the Fevered. If she didn't kill herself, she knew that Darikuto would keep her alive so he could observe her, watch how the infection took her over.

"No," Akalina said. *Whatever it takes* didn't mean throwing her life away at the first chance. "There has to be another way."

Yudur gave her a sly smile. "Are you sure?" he said.

"Is there another way?" Akalina demanded.

"There is," Yudur said. He sounded surprisingly satisfied. "It's a bit harder, but a lot safer for you. Just needed to check that you were of the living, and wouldn't join us at your first chance."

Akalina shivered again. She'd heard people murmur about her, how she appeared as a ghost.

For the first time since she'd realized that her menses would never come, Akalina found herself wanting to live.

"Good," Yudur said, as if he were following along with her thoughts. "Close your eyes and use your landsense to find the center of this place. Then call us to you."

Akalina nodded. The cool ghost hand of Hapta stayed in place, weirdly grounding her as she closed her eyes.

The building in front of her pressed against her senses, as if trying to deflect her. Akalina pushed her senses down, into the soil.

Directly at her feet, the ground felt sterile, as if nothing was allowed to grow there.

That at least made her feel slightly better about Darikuto. He appeared to have set up a barrier deep around the building so that roots wouldn't come poking out.

Pushing through the barrier was like digging through dried land, hard-baked by the sun. It took effort and will. Eventually, Akalina dropped below that, into the sand and silt that formed the next layer. It, too, felt somewhat sterile, though that might have just been the nature of the land itself.

Akalina swam forward through the sand. She found herself imagining her form as a long beam of light with hands and legs to help push herself along.

She could tell the moment she crossed the border of the house itself. The land around her grew moist and warm, like a hothouse. Roots rustled around her, seeking places to grow. They ignored her for the most part, for which she was thankful. She didn't want to have to try to blast her way through them.

It would have been an endless fight, with the roots constantly growing back and adding more tendrils.

The earth was less compact here. It was richer too, as if primed for growing plants.

Akalina concentrated on the heat again, letting it guide her to the center of the area.

A huge round brazier appeared before her. It felt as though it was at least as tall as her physical body was, and that it would have taken half a dozen men with their arms outstretched to reach all the way around it.

Glowing rocks poked out of the top of the brazier. Sparks flew from them, trying to immolate everything. Sigils had been carved around the base of the thing, marks that burned brighter than the rest. She wouldn't allow herself to focus on them, afraid that they'd somehow ensnare her.

The rocks heaved up. Sparks cracked in the darkness. A

huge vine came spewing out. It slithered away to join its companions.

Akalina didn't have eyes to blink, but she felt herself trying to clear them.

Shadows had formed behind the brazier, almost like the ghosts of demons, before they took a physical form.

Akalina split her attention. Part of her stayed focused on whatever that thing was in front of her, as well as the shadows who appeared to be multiplying.

Part of her reached back, calling for the ghosts, for Yudur and Mitolina, for every ghost she could name.

She felt her landsense expand as the ghosts came roaring in along the path she'd laid. A huge army joined her, as deep and as cold of the ocean at her back.

The shadows in front of her wavered for a moment, then they, too, grew stronger. Darker. Blacker.

Leave Yudur whispered in her ear.

Akalina fled back to the surface.

The battle about to take place would last for days, she knew. The two forces would exhaust themselves, bashing against each other.

And for what? What was the end goal?

Akalina found herself alone on the street. No, Hapta was still there beside her.

For the first time she could ever remember, Akalina couldn't sense any other ghosts. They'd all gone under the earth to fight the demons.

How many would survive? She had no idea.

She just knew that she had to stay here, in these lands, until the battle was won, one way or another. Then she could go back to her home, and maybe, maybe, rejoin the living.

Chapter Thirty
HOUSE OF COBALT

❦

FAKRA WOKE up smiling in her tent that morning. There was a good chance that today would be the final day of her cleansing the lands of the House of Cobalt. She'd started three weeks before, at the far eastern border, and had been slowly making her way west.

Cleaning. Blessing. Removing the corruption from the land. Stopping the invasive plants.

Now, she was on the far western border, the part that was adjacent to Darikuto. It didn't surprise her that the plants in this area were the hardest to dislodge.

In other places, the awful vines and poisonous spikes didn't fight her too much. It was like facing warriors who no longer believed in what they were doing, whose heart had left. Or else they were being realistic and understood that their supply chains had been cut.

Here, though, it was like fighting a desperate, cornered enemy who was going to battle to the death.

Too bad that death for all of them was what Fakra had in mind.

And if she could, she'd continue her march, straight into the lands of the House of Pearl.

Not because she felt the need for more land. Quite the contrary. It was going to take a lot of work to maintain the lands she had already.

But she didn't trust Darikuto. Not in the least. She felt better having talked with Chuyoko. Would it be enough, though, when the time came? Or would Darikuto fall prey to the demons, as Kinaki had?

It would be harder to take Darikuto down if he was corrupted further, that would be certain. He knew too much and had too many tricks, being the oldest of the LandHolders. Plus, he wouldn't fall for the same traps they'd used on Kinaki.

No, Darikuto had to be stopped before he started.

And while Yimifut and Unnir certainly had the best of intentions, neither of them had been warriors.

That was the other reason why Fakra waited at the western border. To see if there was need for her to put up a barrier between her land and Darikuto's.

The House of Pearl's lands ran along the entire coast. All the other house lands butted into it. That made it the most dangerous in many ways.

It also meant that it could be invaded from more than one location at the same time. Fakra had laid out plans for the other LandHolders in case it became necessary.

But this morning—one last battle with the remnants of Kinaki's reign.

Fakra got up and immediately started into her morning warrior exercises, stretching and flowing from one position into the next. She'd maintained that discipline since she became a Holder, and saw no reason to stop now.

Step. Punch. Kick. Deflect. Breathe.

By the time Fakra was finished, she was sweating lightly,

but not breathing heavily. Good. She wasn't getting too old for this, though she was in her fifties.

How long before the Land itself abandoned her for someone younger?

Fakra had no idea. However, she was planning on doing all that she could to maintain her house.

For example, she knew that Kinaki had never felt the need to do an annual promenade. The last time that she'd spoken with the other LandHolders in that bedrock room, Yimifut had mentioned that he wasn't planning on a promenade, but a continual cycle through his land.

Fakra had felt the truth of what he'd said deep in her bones.

While she was certain that she'd spend some time in Jinyi, she knew that instead of holding court, she'd be traveling through her land, touching the soil, making sure that the rocks bore her name.

It was going to be more difficult to hold on to the land now. There wasn't as much magic as there once had been. Ghosts had died fighting the demons as well, so there weren't going to be as many auguries either.

Fakra could see a time when she'd be traveling on her own, from Hold to Hold, visiting even the poorest of houses. The people of the House of Cobalt had never placed hospitality as their most important skill before.

That would change. Particularly if you never knew if the stranger at your door might be a wandering LandHolder.

After Fakra cleansed herself and got dressed, she walked out of her tent and into the bright morning sunlight. It was still summer, but the days were growing shorter, the nights, colder. Would she rest when the land did, spend the winter in the city? Then waken and walk with the spring? That didn't feel quite right.

She'd figure it out. The land would tell her, if nothing else.

After eating with the dozen people she'd brought along for the journey, Fakra strode out to the area where she would be concentrating all her powers on that day.

The field looked deceptively clean. Sun-bleached stalks of wheat waved in the slight breeze. Bees buzzed around the purple and pink wildflowers that grew in the shaded patches. Trees lined the edges, a welcome home for the birds and other small creatures.

However, that wasn't what Fakra felt.

Deep under this pastoral vision lay a seething mass of poisonous plants just waiting to break for the surface again. That was part of the problem with the damned demon spoor, it sometimes changed into other things. So it might be corpse flowers. It might be corrupted cornflowers, It might also be those sharp spikes that could impale a warrior's foot if they weren't careful.

Fakra placed her people in a wide circle around the area. If she'd been alone, she would have had a driving line of fire, pushing the plants out.

With this group, she should be able to surround and then uproot the vines before they could spread out.

Fakra pushed out her landsense, touching those around her so that they would know her will.

They would slowly walk toward the center of the field, their combined landsense acting as a net to keep the infection contained.

Then, they'd do battle. Fakra carried her favorite steel digging stick. Others had hoes, poles, even clawed rakes to dig out vegetation.

In the end, she knew they'd be successful. The damned plants didn't stand a chance, though they didn't know that.

Would it be enough if Darikuto fell? How much more

work would be piled on her if he and his lands became corrupted?

She couldn't think of that now. That was a battle for another day.

Today, she had one last skirmish to win for her land.

She smiled again.

Today would be a good day, not just for her, but for the House of Cobalt.

Chapter Thirty-One
HOUSE OF GOLD

❧

UNNIR SAT BACK in her chair, pushing herself away from the maps and notes piled high on the table in front of her.

Before now, no one in the lands had a need for a map. They could just use their landsense to feel what was around them, find their way out of a forest or direct their steps toward a village or a city.

With the magic drained out of the lands of the House of Gold, no one's landsense was as accurate as it once had been. Everyone could find the cardinal points, but that was it.

And these maps weren't just of the House of Gold lands. No, some of them were done in secret, smuggled over from the House of Pearl.

Torja had warned them of what was coming. Vide had already been thinking along those lines, and come up with the plans. Fakra had guided them as well.

Now, they waited for some signal or another that would tell them if they needed to move forward or not. If Darikuto stayed human, or fell to the demons.

"I'm so tired of battles," Unnir complained as she straightened up again.

Vide gave her a sad smile. "I am as well. I am looking forward to retiring to my own Hold one of these days, far outside the city."

"I will come visit you," Unnir said.

"Really?" Vide asked. He seemed surprised. "Why? I would expect you to not want to leave Harvik or your family for a year. Or more."

It made Unnir smile. It was so difficult to surprise Vide. Generally, he'd already thought of everything, as well as all the ramifications of every decision.

"Yimifut brought it up yesterday," Unnir said. She didn't have to explain that they'd been meeting in the bedrock room, as they'd taken to calling it. "He said that an annual promenade was no longer going to be enough to hold on to his land. That he was going to have to cycle through it on a regular basis."

"Interesting," Vide said. He paused, then nodded. "And you are feeling the same, aren't you?"

"I am," Unnir admitted. "I spent a good hour last night just wandering from room to room in the palace, trying to figure out why I was so restless."

At the single eyebrow that Vide raised at her, she gave an exasperated sigh. "No, I'm not pregnant! I wish everyone would stop asking me that."

While she'd certainly enjoyed seeing her husband again, she'd taken precautions to remain childfree. Despite the lack of general magic, it appeared that women still had that ability.

"No, it's because I need to wander the land," Unnir continued seriously. "It calls to me."

"Then go," Vide said.

"But—" Unnir said, indicating the table in front of them, representing their plans.

"Everything can wait half a day while you dip your toes into the soil," Vide said softly. "Even Darikuto."

Unnir blinked. The restlessness took hold again. She felt as though she was trapped in Torja's whirling winds.

"I'll be back by noon," she promised. Then she stood, and took a step out of the room, into the land itself.

Normally, Unnir had a specific destination in mind before she took such a step, so she would know exactly where she was going, whether just a few yards away or several miles.

This time, she let those winds she felt carry her.

With a blink, she realized that she was on the far eastern slopes of her land. She couldn't ever remember traveling such a distance before, particularly without effort.

The hills were covered in sun bleached rocks, white and hot in the clear morning air. No one lived up here. The land was empty, yet full of its self, its own presence pressing around her.

The winds smelled of sweet purple heather. Birds called to each other from the nearby trees. A stream burbled along at her feet. She reached down and dragged her fingers through the cool water, swallowing a mouthful to clear her senses.

She wouldn't have chosen such a place to visit, not for her first call. However, she understood why she needed to be here.

The House of Crystal had its mountains that lay at the heart of it. Yimifut took his power from them, even if much of the land was flat plains.

The lands of the House of Gold were also flat plains, but tipped on either side with mountains. To the east were the veins of precious minerals that the house was named after. To the west was the border of the House of Pearl.

The rocks she stood on held their own counsel, had their own wisdom. They weren't rich with gold. No, they were rich with life, and they far outnumbered the few people who lived there.

Unnir breathed in the baked heat feeling as if it cleansed her soul, burning out places that she hadn't realized had grown dark.

What she'd promised Vide had been true. She would go and visit him. And the other Holds, traveling among the people and binding them to the land as well as the LandHolder.

But she knew she'd spend much more time in places like this, isolated and beautiful, where the heart of her land truly lay.

Unnir looked around for one more moment. Then, with a smile, she took another undirected step, letting the land and the winds choose what she should see next.

Chapter Thirty-Two
HOUSE OF PEARL

꧁꧂

CHUYOKO KEPT her peace as Darikuto laid out the pieces of The New Plan that she would be directly responsible for.

They met in a small room, just the pair of them, the tea on the table in front of them already grown cold. The walls were a soft pink, like scarred skin. They sat on pillows at a low table, Darikuto in his usual robes, while Chuyoko went armorless, just a tunic and trousers, a single knife at her waist.

Darikuto still sought to tame the power of the demon spoors. He was planning on allowing an area of the lands of the House of Pearl to remain infected, primarily the southern-most tip. It would work as an effective barrier for the barbarians down there as well as be out of the way.

He would have magical shields around the land to keep it contained. However, he also expected her to provide guards, so that people wouldn't accidentally get infected.

That didn't sound sensible to Chuyoko. Not in the least. She'd seen how well his plans had worked before—how he'd been far too successful at infecting the land, without acknowledging how much work it would be to contain it.

Plus, what people was he concerned with? Weren't her warriors also people?

"What happens when one of the guards becomes Fevered?" she asked. She picked up her cup just so she had something to hold, so she wouldn't be reaching for the dagger at her waist. Because she knew it would be a "when," not an "if."

Darikuto gave her a cold look. "You'll just have to take care of them. Like you did during the battles at the House of Gold."

"Of course," Chuyoko said, the words forming automatically.

She couldn't allow him to see her internal turmoil. Didn't he understand how awful that had been? To have to kill her own warriors rather than allow them to be taken by the demon spawn?

This was not something she wanted to continue to do. It was one of the few things in her life that had fully shaken her, to the point that she occasionally still had nightmares about it.

Darikuto had other plans, guards at the border, more spies. Chuyoko listened and nodded, asking the appropriate questions when called on.

She had enough discipline to appear as if everything was normal.

However, she couldn't help but think of the warning Shimokoro had given her. How eventually, Darikuto would fall.

Fakra, too, had warned her.

Chuyoko had spent that morning at the oceanside, as always. But instead of doing her warrior exercises, she'd sat and meditated. The winds from the water had been particularly fierce and cold, as if warning anyone back from the waves. At the same time, the sun had seared her back, overheating her.

Too hot. Too cold. All at once. Stuck in the middle of those two extremes, while waiting for that signal, that definitive sign, that it was time for her to act.

Chuyoko had learned patience at Darikuto's side. All that training for the final battle, when he would become the sole LandHolder.

What battles lay ahead now? Battles with demons? With her own warriors?

No. None of this was right.

Darikuto continued talking, spinning out his grand schemes. How he was planning on using Menhaptu to corrupt Yimifut's court. How he'd already started probing Chaotu and Lijun, seeing if he could turn them against Unnir.

Finally, Darikuto appeared to wind down. Chuyoko even managed to smile at him. "Will there be anything else?" she asked.

"No, that will be all," Darikuto said. "Thank you."

No other words of encouragement or praise were given. Darikuto had given his orders. He expected them to be followed.

"Good night, then," Chuyoko said, standing. She passed behind Darikuto as she walked toward the door.

"And goodbye," Chuyoko added.

Without thought, without any warning, she drew her dagger and plunged it into Darikuto's back.

"What?" he said. His magic concentrated on the spot where he'd been injured.

Chuyoko grabbed his head and jerked it hard to the side, breaking his neck.

The LandHolder could not recover. His injuries were too great, as well as too specific. He died with his eyes open, the accusation of disloyalty that lay there burning into Chuyoko's soul.

There was nothing else she could have done, though. He would have betrayed all of the House of Pearl.

She drew out the knife from his back, using what little landsense that she had to feel how the Land had fled from him, making sure that he was finally dead.

Then she slit her own throat, not willing to live with what she'd done, no matter how her hand had been forced.

Epilogue One

HOUSE OF PEARL

The Land itself felt betrayed. Its LandHolder had plans for corrupting it.

Corrupting it!

Not cleaning and cherishing it. Not nurturing it.

Corrupting it.

No single LandHolder would ever have that chance again.

Long lines of ghosts had formed across the width of the land. Chains of chilly presence that started at the borders of the other houses in the east and ended with the ocean.

Instead of a creating a mantle and wrapping itself around a single LandHolder, the Land stretched out. It spread its awareness from the jagged mountains of the north to the steaming jungles in the south. It grew thin in places, like the shifting lands near the ocean where solid land grew capricious.

For a moment, it banded itself together, a solid hard presence. People who were more sensitive felt as though a dark cloud had settled overhead, just above the trees, while the earth beneath their feet had grown hollow.

The moment extended, tension gathering.

The Land could choose to collapse at this point, smothering everything below it. Commit suicide by destroying everything living.

Instead, the Land shattered itself, primarily along the lines the ghosts had formed.

Mountain air rushed in from the northern third, as Yimifut claimed the portion there. The hills grew sharper and the ocean more wild. It would never be like the rest of the lands of the House of Crystal, it would always have its own character. But it would no longer be like the rest of the lands along the coast, either.

The middle section grew milder as Unnir spread out her roots. The hills flattened though the sharp rocks that studded parts remained. Grasses sprouted everywhere, and the winds blowing from the ocean grew softer. In many ways, this land would be the easiest to live in, temperate and warm. But the House of Gold had its own penalties as well.

The southern-most section grew warmer under Fakra's influence. More trees took over the southern-most border, the jungle expanding inward, though still tamed by Fakra. It would be a dangerous place to stay, with shifting land. The waters grew warmer as well, and breakers formed outside the seaports, taming the waves.

There were no longer four Houses, but three, by the time the transformation was complete, each of the remaining Houses claiming part of what had been the House of Pearl's lands.

The one remaining characteristic of the people who remained in the lands of the former House of Pearl was a sorrow that sometimes overcame them. The music they performed remained mournful, even on happy occasions.

And sometimes the Land itself sighed, as if it

remembered what had been, or what might have come, no one was really certain.

Epilogue Two
HOUSE OF GOLD

Vide sat in his study, writing out his latest history of the battles. That fool Kalip thought that he had a cogent analysis of the final days. Ha! Vide couldn't wait to take him apart. Idiot hadn't been there. Didn't know what it had been like. How desperate they'd been, snatching at any and all straws.

Didn't know what it was like to lose someone in a battle. For an armchair warrior like Kalip, it was all theoretical.

The door to his study opened and Lijun poked her head in.

As always, Vide felt a smile cross his face at the simple sight of her.

He'd expected to be alone once everything had settled, particularly after Emil had been killed. Instead, he'd found someone to share the quiet of his days and to warm his nights.

Lijun was the only one who understood his grief. She hadn't lost a brother, but instead, her land. There were days when Vide would admit that her loss was just as devastating as his, when he would be supportive in the face of her anguish.

Then there were other times when Lijun acted as the solid bulwark he could tie himself to as the winds of loss and heartbreak lashed him.

Lijun smiled back at Vide, as if reading his thoughts. She possibly did. They would spend days with very few words passing between them, yet at the same time, still feeling more connected than ever.

"This office needs to be cleaned," Lijun said with fake severity.

"Don't you mess with my papers," Vide warned, as he always did.

Sure, there were stacks of papers and scrolls piled on every horizontal surface. Recently drawn maps hung on the walls. A few potted plants sat neglected in the corner. The shade was drawn on the window at his back, hiding his view of the lovely garden that spread out from the house.

"It's time for lunch," Lijun said, still standing there instead of sitting in one of the chairs next to the desk.

"I'll be there in just a bit," Vide said. "I just want to finish this thought."

"And then there will be the next thought, and the next one," Lijun said. "And it will be sunset and you will be starving and cross as a bear. No, my love. Come now and eat. Then spend some time with me in the garden."

Vide sighed as he put down his pen. "You know, it's insufferable how right you are, sometimes," he said, standing and stretching his arms up above his head.

He had been sitting for some time. He reached out with his landsense and pulled up a small dash of power from the earth, working out the kinks in his back and stretching out his cramped fingers.

Now, it was Lijun's turn to give a wistful sigh.

Vide nodded, understanding. He came around his desk and gently turned Lijun around, so her back was to him.

Then he brought up another trickle of power, sending it coursing down his hands and fingers and into her shoulders and back, relieving all the little hurts and aches that had accumulated over time.

Lijun couldn't draw on the land as he could. It wasn't because of her status as a former inhabitant of the House of Cobalt. No, it was because most people, now, had so much less of a connection to the land than they once did. And there was so much less magic, as well.

People were having to learn all new skills. Candle and lamp making were now things, when before anyone just had to use a touch of magic to bring light to a dark room. Same with using actual wood for fires and cooking.

It took more work, but Lijun claimed to be prouder of the results.

It seemed like far too much effort to Vide. He'd rather spend the time developing and maintaining his landsense, so that the land would continue to support him.

Though that wasn't enough for some people. It was as if the land was no longer tamed and willing to do the work the living directed it to do.

Vide understood that the land still felt betrayed. Though it had been Kinaki who had initially betrayed it, that Darikuto had planned on a similar betrayal had been enough to make the all the lands mistrust the living.

He would leave the arguments about how to rebuild that trust to the philosophers and others who didn't have the rigorous discipline that he and his fellow historians had. They dealt with facts, not fanciful propositions.

Well, at least *he* did. He couldn't always say the same for the others in his field.

"So tell me all about the idiot while you eat," Lijun said, drawing forward and catching Vide's hands in her own.

He looked down, abashed. He hadn't meant to be

muttering out loud. He'd just gotten into the habit when he'd been on his own, before Lijun had joined him out at the Hold Unnir had granted him.

"Of course, my love," Vide said. He paused, drawing Lijun's hands up to his mouth and kissing the fingertips.

"I am lucky, you know," he said softly.

"No, I am the luckier of the pair of us," she insisted as she always did. "Let's argue about it more over lunch."

Vide knew that she was being insistent for a reason, otherwise he'd dillydally through the entire day.

"Fine, lead the way," he said with false exasperation, as he always did.

Lijun grinned, then instead of heading toward their small kitchen with its eating nook, she led him to their bedroom. "Maybe it's time to remind you that you don't need to work all day," she stated.

"I approve of your reasoning," Vide said, smiling as he started to undress.

Yes, he still had pain and sorrow. The land had changed, and nothing was ever going to be the same again.

But he had love now in his life, enough to remind him to live and not just work all the time.

Life was good.

Epilogue Three
HOUSE OF COBALT

Wanho awoke in the underworld. It felt the same as it always had, dank and dark. His rooms were carved out of solid stone, and there would never be any hearth fires to warm it, no lamps to disperse the gloom.

As he rose from the ground, he noticed that his body had changed. He hadn't always been a huge demon. No, he'd accumulated power over time, as well as followers. Those had filled him up, allowing him to grow strong as well as big.

Now, his body resembled that of one of the living, short and scrawny. He couldn't just think his muscles larger, his chest broader, or his legs stronger.

No matter. He would build up his own group of warriors again, until he reached the point of challenging the heavens by stepping back out into the lands of the living.

But this time, he wouldn't be banished. No, he'd find some way of living there without having to rely on a puny person, such as Kinaki.

"You're awake."

Wanho started. He turned to find a small woman standing just a few feet away from him. He instantly envied her muscles and the large sword she carried easily with one hand, though most would need two in order to wield it properly.

"I am Chuyoko," she said with a slight nod. "The Goddess Morta has sent me here."

"The Goddess?" Wanho said. Rage choked his throat. "You actually saw her? Met her?"

"Yes," Chuyoko said with a small, private smile. "She was just here. You were sleeping."

Wanho couldn't help the loud roar of pain that seemed to leap out of him.

He'd battled down here in the underworld for so long, doing the duty that she'd set for him.

But she'd abandoned him, never coming to praise him for doing such a good job.

Chuyoko narrowed her eyes at him and said, "You lack discipline."

Wanho took a step back, as if the tiny woman had slapped him across the face. Then he came roaring back, marching over to where she stood. "I will break you into small pieces," he promised.

"We will fight, yes," Chuyoko said. "Every day. That is my duty, what the goddess had assigned for me. To battle with you, and keep you here. Contained."

Wanho couldn't help the growl that came out. "You won't last," he sneered. "The same battles. Day after day. You'll grow tired, as I did."

Chuyoko nodded to herself, sliding her sword easily into the scabbard at her back. Then she stepped out and did… something. It happened so fast Wanho wasn't certain how she'd hit him, managing to not only make him stagger back, but fall on his ass.

"You lack discipline," Chuyoko told him again. "I do not. Come. Let us begin."

Wanho felt a soul-shaking shiver overcome him. The strength in her voice was harder than any steel.

He had planned on bringing the underworld to the land of the living.

Though Chuyoko was dead, a demon like himself, he'd never think of her that way.

Instead, the living had come to him. And he would learn anew what nightmares were. For the rest of his existence.

Epilogue Four

HOUSE OF CRYSTAL

Menhaptu stood at the top of the stairs leading down to the Chamber of Crystals. Cool air flowed up from the underground cavern, stale and foreboding. He felt awkward standing there in his most formal robe.

Not because it no longer fit his body, but it seemed to no longer fit his station. He juggled (juggled!) crystals now in order to get a decent foretelling. The stiff collar and fabric wasn't appropriate.

Still, as he was going down to the chamber with the LandHolder, he'd thought he'd dress up a little.

Yimifut came walking down the hallway, talking with Akalina, his Ghost Holder.

Menhaptu couldn't help but shiver at the sight of her. She had come back to the House of Crystal after the House of Pearl lands had broken apart, full of stories of the transition.

She, too, had appeared to go through a transformation. On the one hand, she seemed much more alive now, as though she'd more fully stepped into the world of the living.

On the other hand, Akalina had a glow to her now, like a

ghost. The only person in the entire land more powerful than her was Yimifut, and sometimes Menhaptu had doubts about that. She was an odd girl, growing into an odd woman.

There would never be another like her, of that he was certain.

Akalina merely smiled and nodded at him as she approached, before walking past him and onto whatever it was that a Ghost Holder did.

Menhaptu stared after her for another moment, attracted by all that power, yet at the same time, repelled by it.

Yimifut clearing his throat brought Menhaptu back to the present. He could help but compare his formal robes with the outfit Yimifut had on. He wore a typical brown shirt that was cut from blocks and not fit to his body, with green wool trousers and plain sandals.

Yimifut didn't say anything, just gave him a sharp nod. "Right, then. Are you ready?"

Menhaptu sighed. "I am, LandHolder."

Yimifut called up a small ball of light in his hand, then set it to float above his head.

Menhaptu managed to contain his sigh at the ease with which the LandHolder used magic. Very few people had casual magic anymore. Instead, they used candles, and torches, and burned wood in hearths and stoves.

Nothing was the same anymore. Not all of it was Yimifut's fault. Menhaptu knew that. He understood that all the LandHolders had done what they'd needed to do in order for the lands to survive.

If he sometimes grew nostalgic, well, he was allowed.

Yimifut started down the steep stairs of the chamber first. Menhaptu followed directly behind, not wanting to have to try to find his own way through the dark.

The air was even colder down here than he remembered. But at least it wasn't as viscous as it once had felt. The dark was just that—the blackness of an unlit space. It didn't appear to eat at the light as it once had.

Menhaptu breathed a sigh of relief once he stepped off the stone staircase and onto the dirt. It was as if his landsense was stronger down here. He almost felt back to normal.

Almost.

Yimifut made his way forward to the Chamber of Crystals without hesitation. Menhaptu followed, pleased that he didn't need the light as much. He could have found his own way through the dark, the warmth of the chamber guiding his steps.

As they approached, the chamber lit up in greeting. Red, blue, gold, and green light spilled out of the round entrance, across the dirt floor. The lights undulated slowly in a wavy pattern that suddenly grew faster as Yimifut doused his light and stepped into it.

It was as if the chamber only now realized that the LandHolder had come to visit.

Again, Menhaptu swallowed his jealousy. The chamber was never that excited to see him. Then again, he came down here every ten days, so it wasn't as if the chamber really missed him.

Menhaptu stayed outside for a moment, allowing the chamber to greet the LandHolder.

The chamber itself was round, like the inside of a geode. Spikes of crystals stuck out from all surfaces, from the size of a man's fist to the tall ones bigger than a young man. Lights filled the chamber, ranging from the softest white to the darkest blue. A trilling sigh went through the space.

Was the sound louder inside the chamber? That had always been a question for the ages: how much of the song of the crystals was inside the viewer's head, versus actually made out loud?

Yimifut turned to look back at Menhaptu, then gestured him to come into the chamber as well.

Menhaptu was pleasantly surprised when the chamber started up with another round of bright lights. It wasn't as long of a display as when the LandHolder had stepped in. It still warmed his heart.

Maybe the chamber had missed him.

No one ever touched the crystals. They were too sharp. Just touching one left deep cuts.

However, they no longer responded to a single question anymore. They needed more. One of the reasons why Menhaptu waited ten days between visits was because his hands were always cut up by the time he'd finished his visit.

Today, Yimifut was the one who reached out and touched the crystal that was closest to him. It jutted up to about Yimifut's chest. It was hazier than most, instead of a clear crystal it was skimmed over with white. Almost as if a light snow covered it.

Yimifut hummed as he put his palm on the top of the crystal. A trickle of blood immediately flowed down the edge.

Menhaptu didn't hear the response the chamber gave to Yimifut. However, he did see the results.

Crystals pulled back in front of them, showing a pathway through to the heart of the chamber.

Yimifut gestured for Menhaptu to go first this time while he healed the cuts on his hand.

Menhaptu walked gingerly forward, trying to not brush his robes against the edges of the walkway, where the cloth was sure to get cut to shreds.

Ahead, though, was a sight that filled Menhaptu with delight.

It had taken months, but slowly, surely, the Chamber of Crystals had healed, until now, there were no brown or cracked crystals remaining. The chamber was no longer infected at the heart of it.

"Good," Yimifut said when he saw what Menhaptu was looking at. "You will need to stay vigilant," the LandHolder added. "Check on this area regularly. It will be the first sign of something going wrong. Teach your heirs to always check."

Menhaptu nodded. He'd already updated the books that Haptomi had kept, about how to approach the chamber, how to work with it.

Most of what Menhaptu's predecessors had written no longer worked anyway. And it was about time to clear out all that fussiness.

Including wearing formal, floor-length robes that the crystals would casually cut to shreds. No, short pants from now on would be the outfit of the head of the Temple of Truth.

Yimifut turned around and started walking back toward the opening of the chamber.

Menhaptu paused for a moment. He closed his eyes and felt the pressure of the chamber pushing slightly against his skin.

It didn't matter that this was the LandHolder who was waiting for him. Menhaptu had a higher duty to fulfill.

He reached into his pockets and took out the three small crystals that he carried with him always now.

He felt more than heard the rippling sigh of approval from the chamber around him.

Menhaptu opened his eyes and began to juggle. The lights in the chamber flashed more brightly, a type of applause.

He didn't bother to count his throws. He wasn't actually trying to foretell anything. Instead, this was as much about showing his appreciation for the chamber, trying to show how he valued it.

Though he didn't say the words, he let them infuse his entire soul.

Never again.

The chamber, like the land, would never be taken for granted again.

He finished with a flourish and a bow, then followed the LandHolder out of the chamber and back into their new life, their new lands, their new world.

Cast List

HOUSE OF CRYSTAL

Nyati—Capitol
Yimifut—LandHolder
Ibitsima—Former LandHolder
Menhaptu—Current head priest of the Temple of Truth
Haptomi—Former head priest of the Temple of Truth
Akalina—Related to Ibitsima, the former LandHolder
Befery—Akalina's sister
CrsytalHolders—leaders of House of Crystal warriors
Baka—Head of the CrystalHolders

HOUSE OF COBALT

Jinyi—Capitol
Kinaki—LandHolder
Wanho—LandHolder's Demon
Belam—Former head priest of the Temple of Truth
Sunli—Current head priest of the Temple of Truth
CollierHolders—leaders of House of Cobalt warriors

. . .

HOUSE OF GOLD

Haravik—Capitol

Unnir—LandHolder

Torja—Head Priestess of the Temple of Truth

Ragna—Torja's assistant

Chaotu—Son of the House of Cobalt's LandHolder

Lijun—Daughter of the House of Cobalt's LandHolder

Emil & Vide—Cousins of Unnir, children of Yudur, the former LandHolder

VeinHolders—leaders of House of Gold warriors

HOUSE OF PEARL

Yawatan—Capitol

Kinaki—LandHolder

Shimokoro—Head of the Temple of Truth

Benitoyo—Merchant and spy

Chuyoko—Head of the warriors

Orinmegu—Chuyoko's second in command

PearlHolders—leaders of House of Pearl warriors

Read More!

Be sure to pick up all the books in the Houses of the Dead trilogy!

Houses Divided
Houses Fallen
Houses Reborn

Available at your favorite retailers!

About the Author

Leah Cutter writes page-turning fiction in exotic locations, such as a magical New Orleans, the ancient Orient, Hungary, the Oregon coast, rural Kentucky, Seattle, Minneapolis, and many others.

She writes literary, fantasy, mystery, science fiction, and horror fiction. Her short fiction has been published in magazines like *Alfred Hitchcock's Mystery Magazine* and *Talebones*, anthologies like Fiction River, and on the web. Her long fiction has been published both by New York publishers as well as small presses.

Find Leah's books on Knotted Road Press at (www.KnottedRoadPress.com)

Follow her blog at www.LeahCutter.com.

Reviews

It's true. Reviews help me sell more books. If you've enjoyed this story, please consider leaving a review of it on your favorite site.

Come someplace new...

Are you a traveler? Do you enjoy exploring strange new worlds, new cultures, new people?

Journey into the various lands envisioned by Leah Cutter.

Sign up for my newsletter and I'll start you on your travels with a free copy of my book, *The Island Sampler.*

I will never spam you or use your email for nefarious purposes. You can also unsubscribe at any time.

http://www.LeahCutter.com/newsletter/

About Knotted Road Press

Knotted Road Press fiction specializes in dynamic writing set in mysterious, exotic locations.

Knotted Road Press non-fiction publishes autobiographies, business books, cookbooks, and how-to books with unique voices.

Knotted Road Press creates DRM-free ebooks as well as high-quality print books for readers around the world.

With authors in a variety of genres including literary, poetry, mystery, fantasy, and science fiction, Knotted Road Press has something for everyone.

Knotted Road Press
www.KnottedRoadPress.com